THE WHISPERING TREES

ALICE ALLAN

Disclaimer

This is a work of fiction: all characters, events, and locations are fictional or are used in a fictional setting.

A Note About Poisons 💀

There are a number of mentions of the use of natural poisons within the book, notably henbane and fly agaric. This is not intended to imply that using such substances, in any way shape or form, is safe or advisable. Indeed, these substances can be dangerous or even fatal if ingested. Please do not use any of these substances, or infer that they may safely be used, based on their use in this fictional work.

Cover art by Claire Armitage
Edited by Dave Holwill and Sarah Dawes
Layout and design by Oliver Tooley
Typeface Minion Pro 11pt

Published by Blue Poppy Publishing,
87 High Street, Ilfracombe, Devon EX34 9HG

ISBN: 978-1-83778-033-4

A CIP catalogue record for this book is
available from the British Library.

For dear Paul, and her house on the side of the hill.

1 – Widdershins

We were only ten minutes from the new house, the removals van disappearing around the bend of the winding road ahead of us, when Mum blurted out, "Stop the car, I'm going to be sick."

She stumbled out to puke in a ditch.

That was when I saw it. The hill.

All around, the landscape was like the scene on some postcard: hedges, woodland, red ploughed fields, green meadows dotted with tiny black-and-white cows. The hill was different. It rose up out of the surrounding countryside like an island, topped with a cluster of dark trees. It was bleaker, more wild looking. The funny thing was, the more I looked at it, the more I got the feeling I'd seen it before. That was impossible – I'd never been this far west. So why did it feel so familiar? It was silhouetted against the bright autumn sky so that when I closed my eyes it stayed behind my lids in a negative image. I opened my eyes; the trees on the top were now a flaming beacon in the sun.

Mum climbed stiffly back into the car, dabbing her mouth with a tissue.

"Well, Liv," asked Dad, "You always said you wanted to live in the countryside. What do you think?" Despite his exhaustion, the big bags under his eyes, and his sunken cheeks, he looked hopeful.

"It's really pretty," I answered quickly. I turned back to look at the hill, covering my face with my long hair so he wouldn't see my expression. The landscape was beautiful, but there was something about it that made me feel uneasy, something I couldn't put into words. Something brooding.

"Gosh, I hadn't realised Axcombe was quite so far from the nearest town," Mum muttered, her face grey. "How am I going to get to the shops if I run out of milk? You'll have a horribly long journey to school, Olivia. And it's going to take ages for me to make the trips back to London to see Amber."

"Yes, well, it's a shame Amber didn't want to join us in Devon," said Dad tersely, restarting the engine. "Still, I'm sure she'll be fine in London. She's an adult now, and she's got her friends and her new job after all. This is a new start for us. A chance to put my accident behind us and move forward. Let's not forget that, shall we?"

He put a hand out to cover Mum's, but she pulled it away, crumpling up her tissue into a tight ball.

We set off again. Dad's lips were a thin line. Mum patted her blonde bob into place and stared blankly ahead of her. I craned my neck round, watching the hill recede through the back window.

)O(

The new house was smart and bland, just like the London one. Beige walls, beige carpets. There was even a new cream sofa, the kind you could never really relax on in case you got dirty marks on it. Mum had had it all kitted out from a catalogue before we arrived. She'd made it look like something in an estate agent's window so it would be easy to sell when she finally managed to persuade Dad to move back to London.

The removal men started unloading. Dad hung back. I saw him touch Mum's sleeve.

"Sorry. I can't do this," he mouthed to her, before disappearing upstairs. He couldn't face people, social situations. He got panic attacks. PTSD, they called it. Post-traumatic stress disorder. Brought on by the accident that ended his career as a police officer. He'd hide upstairs until they were gone and then come down feeling disgusted with himself.

It wasn't the best start to our 'fresh start'. Mum looked a bit gutted, but she soon put on her 'coping face' and followed the removal guys about, making sure they didn't tread mud onto the carpets. I tried not to get in the way.

As soon as the removals van had left and I'd checked that all the boxes with my precious science books in had arrived safely, I found I couldn't wait any longer.

"I'm just going for a walk," I called.

"Don't get lost, Olivia." called Mum weakly, collapsed on her immaculate sofa. "You don't know the way. The phone reception's terrible. What would Dad say? If something happened—"

But I was already out of the door. I set off in the direction of the hill. For God's sake I was nearly fifteen, old enough to go for a walk on my own. I could hear my sister's mocking voice: 'Plain Jane super-brain. You wouldn't last a minute in the real world.' But her world, London, wasn't the real world, whatever that was. It certainly wasn't my world. I felt trapped by the tall buildings, jostled by the people, choked by the fumes. Like Dad said, I'd always dreamt of living in the countryside, being surrounded by animals, maybe even, although I daren't quite say it aloud, maybe even becoming a vet … One day. I kept my eyes focused on my destination.

Deepest Devon. It sounded like the kind of place you'd have to hack through thorn bushes to get to, but here it was, all patchwork and perfect, a glint of sea in the distance, lit by the low golden sun. It was so good to be walking on soft green verges instead of hard grey pavements. Being by myself made me feel energetic. I hadn't brushed my hair, and I was wearing old trainers, ripped jeans and a skanky old T-shirt that showed off how skinny and flat-chested I was. But here in the countryside it didn't matter. No one was looking. Mum was right, I didn't know the way, but the lanes seemed to funnel me towards my hill. I climbed over a gate and headed upwards, through a field of long, dusty grass. There was a little stone cottage on the hillside below me, with smoke drifting from its chimney.

Looking up, to the summit of the hill, I caught a glimpse of something white between the trees – the walls of an old house? I felt sure I could see something up there, hidden by the dark mass of branches. For some reason, I shivered. That same strange feeling of déjà vu. Why did I feel I knew this place? 'Silly,' I told myself. I tied my hair in a knot at the back of my neck and got ready for the final climb.

I was nearly at the top. I glanced back down towards the cottage. It was only then, out of the corner of my eye, that I saw the figure standing in the doorway below me. The man, or woman, I couldn't be sure, seemed to be screening their eyes from the sun as they watched me. I flinched back, raising my hand in a half-hearted apology in case I was trespassing.

Suddenly, a sharp whistle pierced the air and a huge grey dog came charging from behind the cottage, barking like crazy. It threw its whole body against the fence. I stumbled back in shock.

The dog planted its feet on the top rung of the gate; even at a distance I could hear it slavering and snarling. It looked big enough to jump over if it wanted to. My heart was banging. A dog like that should be tied up! The last thing Dad needed, the last thing I needed, was for me to get mauled on my first day in the countryside. It would prove Mum right about everything, and she'd have us back to London before we knew it. The dog was growling now, a low rattle that I could hear even at this distance. It sounded like it was waiting for the order to attack. I backed slowly away, back the way I'd come, on shaky legs. The figure started shouting something in a shrill, high voice, calling the animal off I hoped. As I edged back, I strained my ears to make out the words. When I did, I got a shock that sent me scrambling down the hill away from the cottage.

"Get out. Get out. Get out!"

2 – When the Lady's Moon Is New

I got back to the new house out of breath, scratched and humiliated. Fortunately, Mum was having a nap and I was able to tidy myself up before supper. Bloody dog. Bloody irresponsible owner. 'Thanks for the welcome.' I thought. For the first time in my life, I had a bit of freedom and I wasn't going to let some stupid yokel scare me off. There was something up there, hidden by those trees, and I was going to find out what it was.

Next day, in the school car park, I bit my fingernails in the front seat of our car, waiting for the bell. Mum was right. Otterton Comprehensive was a long way from the village. In our car, it had taken us twenty minutes to get here, but it was nearly forty by school bus, apparently. I was nervous. I was too much of a geek to fit in at my London school, but at least I'd not stood out. Here, I felt like a foreigner. 'A new start,' I told myself, but my insides were churning.

Mum was frowning into the rear-view mirror, prodding at her hair. I'd told her I didn't need a lift, that I'd rather get the school bus, but she'd stuck her lip out and Dad had lost his temper and shouted at me to stop being difficult. Once a police officer, always a police officer. I did what I was told. It was like walking on eggshells with Dad sometimes.

"Needs a cut," Mum sighed. "Highlights are growing out too. D'you know, I've been going to see Sandra once a month for nearly twenty years. No one knows my hair like she does. I suppose I'll have to risk one of the local salons. Although, I could combine a trip to see Amber in London with a visit to Sandra's. Hmm, I wonder if she could fit me in."

She was scrolling through her phone, looking for Sandra's number, when the school bell went and she remembered where she was.

"Oh, sorry, love. Well, you have a good day at school. You go get 'em and tell me all about it when you get home. All the gossip, who's hot and who's not?"

Half-heartedly attempting to tease me, she poked me with a long fingernail and it hurt.

"Ow," I snapped.

She looked right at me then, defeated.

"I've got a lot on my plate right now, Livvy," she said. I understood. She meant Dad. I wasn't to give her any grief.

"Don't worry about me, I'll be okay," I told her. I gave her a dry peck on the cheek, took a deep breath, and went off to find my classroom.

)O(

"Anning?"

"Sir."

"Bagwell?"

"Sir."

"Crang?" …

I stood at the teacher's desk, trying to hide behind my curtain of hair, listening to the register. There were lots of old-fashioned farmers' names on it. Most people ignored me, but this boy with sandy-coloured hair was staring right at me, drumming on the desk with his fingers. I glanced round the room. One of the girls stood out. She sat by herself, twirling one of her red corkscrew curls, absorbed in a book she was reading. The teacher coughed to get her attention.

"Sadie, this is Olivia, our new girl."

The girl jerked her head up as if she'd been electrocuted, clocked me and cracked her face into a smile. I surprised myself by grinning back. She pulled out a chair for me and as I sat, she whispered, in a terrible American accent, "You ain't from round here, are ya?"

I shook my head.

"Thank God for that," she continued, in her own accent this time, which wasn't at all Devon. "We could do with some fresh blood."

Before she could go on, the door slammed and we all looked up to see a boy striding in.

"Ah, Mr Enticott, you've decided to join us," the teacher announced in a too-loud voice, nervously ducking behind his desk. "What's the excuse this time? Your dad needed you for ploughing? Hedge cutting? I *was* hoping you'd decide to make a fresh start this term."

The boy ignored him and all our stares as he walked across the classroom to his seat. I couldn't see what he looked like because a long fringe of black hair hung over his face, but even with his shoulders hunched he was taller than the teacher. Then, as he passed, I got a glimpse of his face; he was beautiful. Handsome in a way that kicked plain girls like me in the guts. Even though he was scowling, under his bunched-up brows he had the darkest brown eyes and the longest lashes I had ever seen. And it wasn't just me who had noticed him; you could feel the tension in the room as the girls turned away, pretending they couldn't care less. Sadie tutted like a knowing aunt.

"Robert Enticott. The hottest boy in school. Fancies himself as a bit of a bad boy though. Likes a fight, thinks it's funny to get the whole class into detention. I reckon he's just a grumpy sod. I wouldn't waste your time. Anyway, he's a farmer. They only go out with their own kind. They like to keep it in the family. It explains a lot. Our friend over there for starters," she said, pointing in the direction of the sandy-haired boy who'd been staring at me. I stifled a laugh; the boy was staring into space and picking his nose with one extra-long thumbnail. "Richard Waddington, aka Wadsy," Sadie whispered to me with a raised eyebrow. "Living proof of why you should never have kids with your cousin."

Sadie looked after me all day, guiding me around, pointing out the characters. Which teachers were cool, which ones to watch out for. Thanks to her, school would be okay. I could relax on that score. When I got on the school bus, hot Robert Enticott strode straight to the back and weird Richard Waddington sat next to him and didn't bother me, thankfully. On the drive back to Axcombe, I looked out of the window, daydreaming. I found myself thinking of the hill. And then, suddenly, as the bus rounded the bend, as if I'd conjured it up, there it was. It appeared in the distance, wild, mysterious, the trees on the crest dancing in the low sun. I closed my eyes. I could still see it from behind my closed lids. Like it was somehow inside me, waiting to be discovered.

Dad was in the kitchen when I got home, looking a bit lost. Since he'd left his job, he'd been at home during the day. He wasn't a reader and he didn't much like TV. I had no idea what he did with himself all day. 'Sitting around brooding when he should be getting out and about,' Mum would say. I put the kettle on.

"Your mother has gone to Exeter to buy some tassels for the new curtains," he told me flatly. "She asked me to tell you to unpack all the boxes in your room by the time she gets back. Says it can't wait. She's decided to go up to London to see Amber this weekend and she wants all the unpacking done by then." Message duly passed on, he looked at his feet, as if he didn't now know what to do with himself.

"What did you get up to today?" I asked him, in a bright voice, busy with the tea. He looked at me blankly, as he if was seeing me from a long way away.

"Oh, you know …" he said.

He'd probably been holed up in the dark house all day, feeling sorry for himself. Same, same.

"Here's your tea, Dad," I said, handing him a big cup of the sugary builder's brew he liked. There didn't seem to be much else I could do for him. He nodded with a squint of a smile and took the mug off to watch the news. Perhaps this was what it meant to let yourself go. But where exactly had he gone? Wherever it was, I would have taken him by the hand and brought him back if he'd let me. But he wouldn't let me close enough to try.

While I was unpacking, I came across a map of the area. It must have somehow got in with my books when we packed up. It was an old one that had belonged to my grandparents, who used to take holidays down in Devon when Dad was a child. That was why he'd decided to move here – it was the safest place he could think of, I suppose. My mind turned back to that snarling dog. I hoped he was right.

I spread the map out on my bed. There, at the top of the hill, just above the cottage where the person had shouted at me, was the symbol for a dwelling, and the words 'Rowan House'. So there was something up there. As soon as I could get back up that hill, I would find out what it was. Dog or no dog.

3 – Speak Ye Little and Listen Much

By the weekend, the weather began to turn. The Indian summer was over and thunder was coming.

On Saturday morning, as she packed for her trip to London, Mum fretted. "Trust me to get a migraine when I've got a long train journey ahead of me. You be good and don't get under your dad's feet. You will ring me if he has a bad night, won't you, Olivia? I can come back if he needs me. There's pizza in the freezer. I'll ring you when I get there."

I seized my chance. As soon as she was gone, I was out of the house and walking. After a week cooped up at school or stuck at home unpacking, it was so good to be out, to feel my breath in my lungs and feel my legs working under me. The freedom of being outside and completely and utterly alone was exhilarating. This time I approached the hill from the other direction, out of sight of the cottage. Even so, I walked cautiously, all the while expecting to see that big grey dog racing towards me.

As I approached the summit, I was hot and out of breath. The wind splattered a small squall of raindrops across my face. The old ladies on the beaches in Lyme and Sidmouth would be gathering up their towels and windbreaks and heading towards cafes for their cream teas. A storm was brewing, and far away, over the long ridge that marked the horizon, there was a flicker of light, followed by the growling of muffled thunder.

I'd made it.

As I stood alone on the top of the hill, my hair flying around me so I could hardly see, I should have felt elated. But as I looked around, I felt a bit let down. A single pine, and a circle of dark trees. I don't know what I was expecting, but more than this, anyhow. The leaves of the trees flickered silver in the breeze. Rowans, I decided, remembering Granddad's map. So where was this Rowan House? Keeping out of sight of the cottage below, I crept through dried leaves to a clearing in the centre. And there, hidden amongst a tangle of bracken and brambles, I found what remained of it: a pile of rubble and three bare stone walls, one with an empty doorway. The roof had long since rotted away.

As I circled the ruins, bracken caught at my ankles, and whips of bramble scored my bare arms with beads of blood. A rotting wooden board creaked as I stepped on it, and I jumped quickly aside. Nervously I peered through a crack in the boards; I saw nothing but darkness. A disused well. I picked up a small handful of gravel and tipped it through the crack. I heard it ricochet off the walls before plopping into shallow water at the bottom. It didn't sound that deep; it was probably half full of rubble. Even so, I'd been lucky. If I'd fallen in and got trapped, no one would have known where I was. The thought made me shudder.

I stepped inside the house through the old doorway, hoping for a bit of protection from the anxious wind which had buffeted me all the way up the hill. But, in the sudden eerie quiet, the excitement I'd felt at being alone vanished. The hairs on my arms rose. I stood still and strained my ears listening, but the only sound was my thumping heart, and the sighing of the branches of the pine as the breeze pushed through it. I shivered, shrugging the feeling off.

'*Olivia.*'

I spun round. Someone had said my name, I was sure of it. But the ruins of the old hilltop cottage were empty. The birds had stopped singing now, and through the empty socket of the window, the rowans were dancing. Above, where the roof would have been, the sky was looking sick. The sweat on my back chilled and the walls began to feel like a trap. As I stepped quickly back through the doorway, I glimpsed something moving through the trees: the owner of the hill? Had they seen me? Was it them who had spoken? How did they know my name? Please, let that dog be safely locked up … I held my breath. Whoever it was had disappeared away from me round the side of the building.

I followed, half crouching, trying to stay unseen. Rumbles echoed off the hills. The storm was getting nearer. I tried to think rationally. "Lightning is an electrical discharge between two opposite charged surfaces," I repeated to myself but it didn't do much to slow my heart down. How ridiculous my logic seemed right now. There was no time to be logical. Up here I was an animal, relying on my senses. As the first drops of rain began to fall, I turned to run, but a close thud of thunder jerked the breath out of me and a bracken tripwire sent me sprawling to the floor. My hair caught in the brambles, holding me fast.

'*Olivia!*'

An overpowering smell of mildew, leaf litter, vegetation. This time I felt hot breath right next to my ear, the voice soft but insistent. I couldn't tell if it was male or female; it was cracked and unworldly, the voice of something long-buried that needed to speak. I lurched away from it, ripping my hair from the thorn bush as I pulled free to scrabble on the ground.

"What do you want?" I whimpered. Those tendrils of breath were taking root in my brain; I smacked the side of my head to dislodge them. The trees and walls and storm loomed and boomed above me. Then I saw the little bodies in the undergrowth. Tiny yellow bodies with matted feathers, some with broken necks and some with no heads at all. Hooded eyes and open, sad-clown beaks. At first, I thought I was imagining them, but the sweet stench of their rotting flesh told me otherwise. Rain pelted my head and the wind screamed through the pine. I scrambled to get up and ran from Rowan House, out into the open, across the springy grass and over the hummocks between the trees. I flew down the steep hill, drenched by the summer storm until my momentum overbalanced me and I bowled to the bottom. The fall took the breath out of me. I lay flat on my back, unable to move, the rain falling hard on my face.

4 – Where the Rippling Waters Go

I lay on the wet grass, winded and bruised. Suddenly, someone or something loomed over me. I jerked away, but strong hands reached down, took my arms and pulled me to my feet. Then they guided me down the hill and towards the cottage that I'd run from only a few days before. They steered me towards a stool in an old-fashioned kitchen and pushed me to sit. The owner of the hands wore a man's shirt, and trousers held up with baling twine; it was only when we entered the cottage that I realised she was a woman. She hardly spoke. She kept her head of white curls bowed low and ignored my apologies. She wrapped me in rough wool blankets and rubbed me dry by the range.

It was warm inside and smelled of dog. Three of them trailed anxiously at her heels, the big grey dog amongst them. Up close, the woman was much older than I'd first thought, given her strength. She had a small mouth and fine features, but the wrinkled skin of her face and hands was ploughed and furrowed like a winter field. I couldn't read her expression. She smelled of carbolic soap, creosote and lavender.

"I was on the hill …" I began through chattering teeth.

She stopped rubbing and her bright, hazel eyes fixed on me strangely. Without warning she left me. Her grey dog, some sort of whiskery mongrel deerhound, laid its head in my lap and began to lick my hands like I was its half-drowned puppy. The others – a wiry terrier and a fat old spaniel with misty eyes – came and sat at my feet.

I thought the woman must have gone out to call an ambulance, but she came back a few minutes later with a fistful of something and a jar of honey. She tipped whatever it was into a teacup, added a spoonful of golden honey, and, taking a big old-fashioned kettle from the range, poured hot water over them.

"Drink this," she muttered.

It was not her voice I'd heard on the hill. So, whose voice had it been?

"What is it?" I asked, peering at the pale, yellow liquid in the mug. It smelled of hay.

"Tea. For the shock," she said gruffly, sounding more used to speaking to animals than to people.

I put it to my lips. It tasted bitter and sweet at the same time. I drank it all. The woman pulled up a chair and sat down, saying nothing but waiting patiently as if she expected me to start speaking.

A strange thing began to happen; first of all, my teeth stopped chattering. Then, I started to talk. Perhaps it was the drink she gave me, or maybe it was just the way she listened. In any case, I needed to explain myself, my odd behaviour, the fact that I'd come back to the hill when she'd shouted at me to steer clear, the reason I was lying in a wet heap on the ground. A stream of words flooded out like a river bursting its banks.

I told her about my life in London, my family, Dad's accident. All the dark, unmentionable stuff, all the silt, the dark muddy rubbish that was clogging me up, out it came. And as the words came out, a warm, calm feeling took their place; I felt clean, empty, bright. I babbled on to the sound of rain thrumming on the roof tiles and thunder roaring as it passed over. Drips from the roof cascaded into pots and buckets arranged across the flagstones; the tinkling sounded like strange music. Among the other containers on the floor there was a big silver bowl; what light broke through the scudding clouds seemed drawn to the bowl and was reflected back to illuminate the ceiling in a shuddering disc of light. The water it contained rippled and reverberated with every drip, a magical, hypnotic chime. Every bit of me wanted to reach out and touch it and to stare into the bright depths. Did I tell her that? I know that, eventually, I told her what I'd seen and heard on the hill, because it was then that the woman stood up and went to the window as if she was suddenly short of breath. The rain had stopped and a rainbow flung itself across the grey-bright sky.

"Thank you," she breathed, though it seemed that she wasn't talking to me. After a moment, she turned and looked me up and down, a bit critical. "Well, Olivia White, I been waiting for you. I'm Annie Tilke." She paused, looking suddenly unsure. "You felt something on the hill, didn't you?"

I nodded.

"That's good. You should always trust your intuition." Those hazel eyes bored into me now. "And what you felt, it was uneasy, wasn't it?"

I nodded again and she drew a deep breath as if her fears had been confirmed. "Something's not right. I've felt that for a long time. I've been waiting for some sort of sign. And now you're here. You a good learner?"

"Yes," I replied, wondering where she was going with this.

"Good. Perhaps you'll serve then. I don't believe in coincidence. It's not by chance you've stumbled on my door. I can't say as I can explain what you felt up there, Livvy, but I've lived here my whole life and in time I can learn you a few things that'll help you make sense of it all."

She took the blanket from my shoulders and folded it neatly.

"The rain's easing now. You best get yourself home and cleaned up. But you come back tomorrow and we can talk more. I suppose you've heard what they say about me?"

"No," I said, confused.

"They call me a witch, Liv. And maybe I am, in a manner of speaking."

5 – Let the Spell Be Spoken

Very early next day, I got up, got dressed and set off to see the old woman again. But halfway up that weird hill, I sat in the dewy grass and wondered what on earth I was doing. I looked down the valley, sparkling in the morning sunshine. Was it wanting to belong here that made me feel that I already knew this place? Above me, the ruins of Rowan House hid behind their cloak of trees. I glanced back nervously. Chicks, thunder, silver bowls … Did she really say she was a witch? I had to get things straight with myself, to weigh up just what I was getting myself into, before I went back and spoke to that old woman.

I didn't believe in magic. No sensible person did. I believed in scientific proof and evidence. But I couldn't find any logical explanation for what I'd heard on the hill. Up there, past the boundary of the rowans, things had happened I couldn't explain. Things that didn't fit. I needed some answers and the old lady said she had them. High above me stretched a mackerel sky, and floating below, puffy balls of cotton wool. My sister Amber was right; I was a science geek. Cirrocumulus, cumulonimbus. Naming, explaining, containing. That was how the world made sense to me. But today, those words weren't enough. There were no words in the world to contain all that beauty. It was like I was seeing clouds for the first time.

I saw smoke curling from the chimney of the old woman's cottage and I heard her cockerels crowing. I saw her come out into her back garden, and, though I was far away, I caught the welcoming smell of the fresh bread she had been baking. My mouth filled with saliva. People say instinct is in your gut, but that's not how I felt it. Instinct was the smell of that bread on the breeze, a scent that led me forward.

'It doesn't make sense.' I fretted for a second. Then I took a breath. Before I could talk myself out of it, I scrambled down the hill to the cottage.

Annie Tilke was wearing overalls and there were bits of straw in her white curls. "So, you've come then?" she said tersely. She pointed at her lawn. It was covered in shards of glass. "Look! All my tomatoes. Sliced on the vine. Blooming vandals came up the lane last night. I must be getting deaf. Never heard nothing. You'd have thought the dogs would have barked or something."

"What? That's awful. Who would do a thing like this?"

The metal frame of the greenhouse was a skeleton. Whoever did it had kept smashing until no pane was left unbroken, no pieces of glass were left hanging in the frame.

"Reckon it's village boys, probably. Blighters, they are."

"Have you called the police?"

"No," she replied, "No point. Don't want to make a fuss. An old bird like me, living alone, you've got to keep your head down. I don't want social services up here, poking about, asking me if I wouldn't rather be in a nice little home with the other old folks. No thank you. It's not the first time I've been baited and won't be the last."

She didn't say, but I could guess what they were baiting her for, and it seemed too stupid to be true: for being a witch.

"I'll help you clean up the glass."

"Later, later. Only thing to do right now is put the kettle on and forget about it." She raised an eyebrow and looked me up and down. "Well, Livvy. It's about time you made an appearance."

In the kitchen, great oak beams snaked across the ceiling and there were cool flagstones underfoot. Over a plate of fresh bread and jam and mugs of steaming tea we got talking about the storm that had brought me here.

"Mazed as an adder, you was yesterday," the old lady grunted. "Soaked to the skin too. All better today though?" Her voice fitted this place; her long round vowels sounded like the lowing of cows, but the strong, clipped call of a cattle-herder was in there too. "'Twas a proper summer storm. Blessed roof won't stand too many more like that. I'll run out of bowls to catch the leaks. I thought you were one o' them village louts when I saw you on the hill that first time. I planned to dry you off then send you packing, only you started your blethering. You ain't blethering so much today, though, are you?"

"I was a bit crazy," I admitted.

"And Nellie here wouldn't stop licking you."

"I think she was trying to warm me up."

On hearing her name, Nellie, the big deerhound, started wagging and wiggled over to put her head on my knee. Pip, the terrier, thought he was missing out on something and scuttled over too, pawing with scratchy toes at my legs. Noggin, the poor old spaniel, had cataracts and stiff joints but joined in from his bed by thumping his tail.

"Good thing I like dogs," I laughed. "My sister would be having a screaming fit right now."

"Whereas you, you've always had a way with animals ain't you?" said Annie, fixing me with her bright eyes. "What do your folks make of you wanting to be a vet, then?" she asked.

Damn. I must have confided my secret to her along with all the other stuff I'd told her after the storm. A vet? Me? It was a pipe dream. Mum and Dad would laugh me out of town.

"Oh, they don't know," I answered hurriedly. "I can't tell them. I mean, they wouldn't get it. I don't see how … It'll probably never happen anyway," I muttered.

"Hmm," she mused, eyes bright as a bird's. I didn't like it when she looked at me like that. Like she was trying to see inside me, to piece together the bits of me. Just for a second, I thought I saw something greedy in her expression. But she smiled, and continued sweetly, "Well, maybe later you'll help me with the goats and chickens. You'd like that, would you?"

"Really? That'd be brilliant."

"Good. Well, I reckon you must have a few questions. I know I have. And I reckon the best place for talking is Rowan House."

"Rowan House? But … I'm not sure …"

"No point wasting time," she said, and held open the door.

6 – Bind the Spell Well

We climbed the slope in silence. She was upright for a woman of her years but lugged a stiff hip when she walked.

"What's this flower called?" she asked suddenly, pointing to a tall yellowish flower amongst the grass.

"I don't know. Buttercup?"

"Course it isn't." She snorted. "When I was your age, I knew all the names of flowers and what they were good for. I suppose I'll have to teach you herb lore 'n'all."

"Will you? Why?" I asked.

She tutted impatiently. "It's all connected. Oh, it's no use explaining. You'll see."

I was getting really panicky. I wasn't happy about going back to the place where I'd heard that voice say my name. I needed some answers, about the hill, about the voice, but right now I couldn't even make the right questions. The old lady had fallen quiet, too, but she kept shooting me glances. From time to time, she drew breath and I thought she was going to ask me something. Then she'd shake her head and think better of it.

When we reached the clearing in which the ruined house stood, we stopped. I cast a quick eye over the undergrowth, but I couldn't see any chicks. Nothing out of the ordinary. Perhaps the storm had washed them away. Perhaps some animal had eaten them. For a second, I felt lost, like I was going mad. Were they the work of Annie's village boys? But where would they have got them from and why bring them up here? It was too weird. The old lady reached out a wrinkled hand and laid it on the smooth bark of one of the rowans. She turned her hazel eyes on me.

"Livvy. I ain't about to tell you what to believe."

"Okay," I said, embarrassed. It always felt awkward when people went all earnest.

"First of all, what I said about being a witch. You've got to know it ain't me that calls what I do witchcraft."

"Oh. Okay. What do you call it then?" I tried to pretend she'd told me she was a dentist or a hairdresser or something, like this was a normal conversation.

"Healer or helper, maybe. Something like that. My mother was the same, and her mother before her. Hedge witchery, some folks call it." She fluttered her long fingers like she was waving away the silliness of the outside world. "Oh, but names don't mean nothing. I mark the seasons. I give thanks. I heal and help where I can. And I make charms for people who have need of them."

"When you say charms, do you mean, like ... spells?" I felt stupid even saying the word.

Annie smiled. In a fork between two branches of the rowan hung a spider's web. Gently, she tickled a strand of it and the whole web quivered.

"The way I see it, everything in the universe is connected. Your wishes, wants and desires, your spell, that's the vibration that shivers through the web."

"Right," I muttered. This was nuts, and I was squirming inside. "But, who … what makes the spell work? Or not work?" I added hurriedly, scuffing my feet in the leaves.

"Mother Earth, that's who I look to," she answered unapologetically. "You better believe she's plenty powerful enough." The old woman was looking at me with those bright bird eyes. "Alright. I've given you some answers. Now I've got some questions. Tell me again. Just before the storm, Olivia. What did you hear?"

"I've told you everything already. I heard a voice. All it said was my name. A couple of times. Olivia."

"And the voice. What was it like?"

"I dunno," I replied, feeling stupid.

"Try to find the words."

"It was old. Not 'people' old, but old like a hill, or a stone, or something."

Out loud, it sounded crazy, but she nodded, creeping closer. I shrugged apologetically. Suddenly, two bony hands shot out. I gasped but she held me firmly by the shoulders. Up close I caught the stale smell of old women who live alone: sour breath, lavender, and mothballs.

She spoke quietly but her eyes were hard under her dark brows. "Livvy. There must have been more than that. Come on. Remember. It's important."

"There wasn't." I insisted. I should never have come up here with this crazy woman.

"Come on, girl. There's no time to play games. I need to know. What did you feel when it spoke? Try to think. What was the message?" She shook me hard by the shoulders.

"I don't know," I whined, trying to squirm out of her grasp.

She must have seen I was telling the truth, that she was scaring me, because she let go of my arms and strode off. In the centre of the abandoned building, she stopped and raised her fists up. "Why don't you talk to me no more?" she called to the sky and the treetops. "All these years, I've served you well, ain't I? Why d'you go and leave me now?" She flung an arm in my direction. "And what d'you pick her for? She's too young. There's no time to teach her. Why d'you send her, when her heart's not in it? There's too much at stake to risk it on a child."

She peered expectantly at the sky as if waiting for an answer. Nothing.

Her bony fingers spread wide, stroking the air, and she spoke in a coaxing voice. "Something's not right. Even a fool can see that. You need help. Well, I'm here. I'm still here! Just give me a sign."

Nothing happened. The only movement in the blank blue sky was a tiny white cloud. The name altocumulus pinged pointlessly into my head. Through a gap in the trees, I watched it moving slowly away. I was embarrassed for her. After a while she looked down to the ground; I saw her shoulders droop. Then her whole body crumpled and she knelt in a heap among the leaves.

"Please don't leave me," I heard her pleading to the earth. "They turned their backs on me in the village 'cos of what I do in your name. I can put up with the loneliness as long as you still speak to me. My time's not done yet, is it? Where are you? Where are you?"

The little cloud was long gone by the time she stopped muttering and came to her senses. She looked over to me.

"Olivia, listen. Long before the building of the house were the stones. There's something in the stones of the hill that makes this place special. Magical maybe. When life hangs in the balance, it's said the stones can help. Longer than I can say, people have been coming here to pay their respects to the sun, to the moon, to their gods and goddesses. Bringing their sick to be healed, leaving their offerings, asking their questions. I guard the hill."

"You guard the hill?" I whispered.

"And my mother before me, and before that my grandmother. This land's been in my family since before there was records."

"Guard it from what?"

"There are people who would suck the power out of this place and use it for their own, never thinking of the balance, or what terrible danger comes to all of us if it's lost. They'd come here, Liv, if they got even a hint of the strength stored up here, and before they understood it, they'd waste it away. I'd lay down my life before I'd see that happen." She attempted to get up. "I'm so sorry, Livvy. I should never have asked you what you saw and heard on the hill. I won't do it again. The message was for you, not me. This is your time. You been chosen. You been chosen for a purpose, Liv, for your keen senses maybe. I'll help you the best I can. Here, help me up."

Cautiously I went closer and she put out a hand. All her fierceness was gone and she felt frail.

"Oh, Liv, you're looking at me like I'm stark raving mad and I don't blame you," she said as I helped her down the hill. "I've behaved badly. I'm sorry I frightened you. I hope I haven't frightened you off?"

I shrugged. All this talk of me being chosen made me confused and irritable. I admit it, I felt a spark, a quick burst of excitement when she'd talked about there being a message for me on the hill. I wasn't going to get pulled deeper into some bunch of rubbish I didn't believe in. But … I had heard the voice.

"The voice. What was it?" I muttered.

She shook her head. "Like I said, it spoke to you, not me. No point me telling you what I think it is. It's best you make your own sense of it. Things'll come clear in time, my dear."

We had reached the gate at the bottom of the hill. "Now, tomorrow after school, will you come back to meet the goats?"

7 – Chanting Out the Baneful Tune

Even though the school was new, in the science lab I was back on solid ground. I knew this stuff. Photosynthesis, osmosis, meiosis. My sister, Amber, was always calling me a science geek, but the words made me feel calm. They gave order and structure to the world.

"Olivia, can I have a word?" called Mr Dory, the science teacher, after a biology lesson. He had a kind face with these bushy white eyebrows that climbed up and down his forehead with every thought. By the way they leapt and bounced as he taught you could see he must really love his subject. "I've been told by your last school that you have a talent for natural sciences and I can see it's true," he told me. "How do you plan to use this talent?"

"Um, I don't know yet," I replied, taken aback.

"Well, in the New Year you've got a work experience placement coming up. Don't waste it. In the meantime, I'll look out some more advanced books for you. So you won't get bored in class."

I didn't like to tell him I'd already read most of the A level text books.

I told Sadie what the teacher had said to me.

"Wow. That's so cool, Livia." she thrilled. "You're like some sort of genius scientist, the next Einstein. And this lady Annie, who's teaching you about animals and herbs and stuff, that's going to give you loads of experience too. You're going to be a brilliant vet."

I'd told her a bit about Annie. About the goats and the chickens and the dogs. That was it though. For all that Sadie was a bit of a hippy, I wasn't sure she would handle the weird stuff. Come to that, I wasn't sure I had the words to explain it. I'd sworn Sadie to secrecy about my visits. I couldn't have Mum knowing where I was.

"Me, I don't get science at all, or maths," my friend went on. "Yuck. I'm going to teach English, and make films and write novels. Loads of them. And maybe poetry." She looked over at Robert Enticott and sighed. "Maybe about him ..."

We both gazed at Robert. He was glaring out of the window. His dark hair shone in the September sun. He kept pulling out his mobile phone, scowling at it, then messaging under the desk. He'd rolled up the sleeves of his shirt and you could see the whole length of his brown forearms. The top button of his shirt was undone and he was muscly from all his farm work. I had to look down before he caught me staring.

"He's bloody gorgeous, isn't he?" whispered Sadie without taking her eyes off him. "Shame his personality doesn't match his looks."

Robert was frowning so hard at his mobile I thought he might chuck it across the room.

"And anyway, it's not like he's got much competition," Sadie continued. "I mean, half the boys in our year are more interested in playing computer games than talking to girls, and the other half are such chauvinist pigs that if you even said good morning to them, they'd tell the whole school you tried to chat them up. What can you do? He's a grumpy git, but you have to agree, he is nice to look at."

At lunchtime, Wadsy followed Sadie and me around like a dog looking for scraps. He gabbled when he spoke; you could never really tell if he was talking to you or to himself.

"So, what you got planned after next year's exams then, Liv? You leaving? Nah, you're not thick like me, proper der-brain I am, you're staying on aren't you. I knows, I knows," he leered, tapping his nose and sending himself up. "What you gonna do then, Liv? Business, is it? Make some money? In the city? Yeah, I can see you in a suit, with a waddycall, a briefcase."

"Yeah, right," I muttered.

"Yeah, right." He laughed, like I'd said something funny. Sadie told me not to encourage him or we'd never get rid of him.

The bell for the end of school had just gone and Sadie and I were walking round the back of the gym when Wadsy came charging around the corner without looking. Sadie's books and make-up went flying across the path.

"Oi!" she shouted. "Look where you're going."

"Sorry, Sades, didn't see you." He grinned, rushing back to help her pick things up. "Alright, Liv?" He leered, jigging about on the spot like he needed a pee. "In a hurry, see? There's gonna be a fight, outside the school gates. It's all been arranged. Don't wanna miss it."

"Who's fighting? Why?" asked Sadie.

"Robsy, of course. Steve's come to get his own back. Rob's gonna get mashed." Wadsy rubbed his hands in glee.

"You mean your *mate* Rob? Robert Enticott? You don't seem that worried about it, Wadsy."

"Yeah, well, Robsy likes a good fight. And it's not like he wasn't asking for it."

"It'd be a shame if he spoiled his pretty face," said Sadie to me with a wry grin. She looked nervous though. Perhaps she liked him even more than she was letting on.

"Anyway, you coming? You'll miss it at this rate," Wadsy called back as he ran off.

The fight had already started when we got there. It was in the car park near where the school buses pulled up. Sadie and I stood at the back, gripping each other's arms. Robert and the other guy, Steve, were squaring up to each other, surrounded by a crowd of boys. Steve looked like a blonde gorilla; he was at least twenty and so muscly that his shoulders bunched right up into his neck. Robert's nose was bleeding. He wiped it away with the back of his hand, looking pleased at the sight of the blood. He had a strange half-smile on his lips as he circled the other guy.

"I hope he's not badly hurt," breathed Sadie.

I nodded but I couldn't speak for the adrenaline. I could smell it in the air: sharp, animal. Steve had a big bruise coming up on his cheek; he had his fists up and I could see he was scared. He'd lost his confidence. Robert must have sensed it too because he suddenly launched himself at Steve and began pounding him; he moved so fast it was hard to tell how many of the blows landed home, but soon

Steve had his arms over his head, and it wasn't long before we heard him shouting out in surrender.

"Alright. Alright!"

Wadsy and a couple of other boys jumped in to pull Robert off. Steve's mates hauled him up. They helped him stagger off, shouting abuse until they turned and legged it.

Robert stood panting. His nose was dripping blood and his dark hair stuck to his flushed face.

"Rob, mate, we'd better get out before the teachers get wind of this," warned Wadsy. He tried to lead him away but Robert brushed him off and shook himself down. He was waiting for the teachers. He wanted them to know he'd been fighting. He actually *wanted* to get into trouble.

Sadie took my arm. Wadsy and the other boys ran for it.

"Time we left, too, Olivia." Sadie had backed off.

There was no one left but us, but I was transfixed. I couldn't take my eyes off Robert. For a second, he looked my way and my breath stopped. It was enough to rouse me to my senses. I looked quickly down.

"Come *on*, Liv," urged Sadie. We scuttled off to the bus park just in time. I heard the bellowing voice of a teacher.

"Robert Enticott! Headmaster's office. Now."

8 – Soft of Eye and Light of Touch

The clocks hadn't changed yet and the evenings were still long.
Mum was back with a smart new haircut and news from the big
city. Already, London felt a world away and I wasn't missing it
one bit. Unfortunately, the country air and peace and quiet had
had no effect on Dad. He was still holed up in his room. I told
Mum I was going to meet Sadie for a bike ride after school.
Instead, I cycled over to Annie's.

Annie wasn't in the garden. I went round to her back door.
When I saw what was lying on her doorstep, I stood staring for
a full minute: three dead chicks, with matted feathers and
broken necks, lying in a neat row on her doorstep. Chicks on
the hill, chicks here. What was going on?

'Get a grip, Liv,' I told myself. 'Stop being pathetic. There
must be a rational explanation.' Eventually I steeled myself, and
picked them up one by one, grimacing at the feel of their cold,
stiff legs between my fingertips. I dropped them into Annie's
dustbin and then shook it to make sure they would sink to the
bottom out of sight. Now she would never need to know the
village bullies had paid her another visit.

Annie was cheerful. She kept her promise to introduce me
to her goats. Beryl and Mavis planted their feet on the stable
door and bleated. Their yellow eyes, pupils like post-box slots,

scanned us for treats, and as I learnt how to muck out, I got butted and nibbled. I loved it. After all yesterday's weirdness on the hill it felt real and right. Next, Annie showed me the secret places where her bantam hens laid their tiny blue eggs. Cockerels had competitions to out-crow each other.

"Soft old thing I am, I can't bear to get rid of 'em. Waste of good corn, but I like to watch 'em strut about in their finery. Never needed an alarm clock neither."

Back on home ground, the desperation had gone out of her.

After we'd visited the bees that buzzed in and out of her white-slatted hives, she took me down to the stream below the cottage. She taught me to name the trees that stood by the water's edge and in the wet banks she showed me a new flower.

"Might as well start as we mean to go on. This'll be your first lesson in herb lore. This here's hemp agrimony. We're going to collect it today for drying. Alright?"

The plant grew in a clump which came up to above my knees. It had reddish stems, covered with downy hair and toothed leaves. The flowers were a dull lilac colour, and they grew in masses, with white fluffy stamens. *Pistils*, *petals*, *anthers*; I knew all the words to describe it, but I knew nothing else about it.

"What's it for?" I asked.

"Well, this one's good for fevers and chills, for people and animals. You make it into a tea. But it's a good all-rounder too. You take the fresh leaves, bruise 'em, mix 'em with lard and there's a poultice for you. It'll draw out pus from a wound. Used it on Beryl's leg when she cut it on barbed wire. She was better in no time."

Annie handed me a penknife and showed me how to cut the woody stem near to the ground. The cut plant had a nice meadowy smell. When our arms were full, we walked back across the field to the cottage.

The still room where she kept her herbs was at the end of a long, flagstoned corridor, more of an outbuilding than a part of the house. I opened the latch and light flooded into the corridor. Plants were drying on racks in the window. On the work table stood a heavy pestle and mortar for grinding herbs to powder. The early autumn sunshine lit up shelves and shelves of glass jars, neatly lined up and labelled. Wormwood and coltsfoot, comfrey, skullcap, white willow, motherwort, vervain. The labels were written in different hands. Annie took down one called St John's herb. The label was written in faded brown copperplate.

"My mother's handwriting. She knew more about herbs than anyone before or since. Used them helping mothers in childbirth mostly."

"She was a midwife?"

"Something like that. Bit of everything. In those days it wasn't unusual to give birth at home. Farmers' wives trusted her more than the doctors, and she wouldn't accept no money. Farmers always saw to it that we got eggs and honey though. Got a whole pig once, when she delivered twins." She laughed, remembering.

"And she taught you about delivering babies? And herbs?"

"And the rest. And her mother taught her. So I might as well teach you, since I ain't got no daughter of my own. Now, hand me that hemp agrimony."

We strung the flowers head-down near a window.

"Next time you come, we'll take the flowers off and store 'em for using with the animals."

"It seems like a lot of work. Why not just go to a vet?" I asked.

She tutted impatiently.

"Oh, I dare say medics have learnt a few things since these cures were found, but I dare say they've forgotten a few things too. These plants grow free in the hedges and ditches all round here. People been using them since before there was records. You don't go ignoring what's right under your nose, not if you've eyes to see it, Liv. Not if you know it works."

She lugged down a huge book from a shelf. It was full of illustrations of plants and flowers. The margins were full of notes her mother had made. There were ancient envelopes with scribbled recipes on the back stuffed between the pages, even bits of greaseproof paper with notes on.

"I'm going to feed the goats. You sit here and have a read. Pick a herb from the shelf and read up on it. If you're to be a vet, then most of these cures are good for animals as well as people."

She went out, and I got down a jar of herbs labelled 'Feverfew'. It was a light green powder, with a strange, exciting smell. I leafed through the tattered pages of the book looking for a reference. I was flattered Annie would try to teach me. There was something satisfying about the idea that this knowledge had been handed down between generations. It was full of fascinating facts, but more than that it was practical, full of stuff you could apply to real life. And, of course, there wasn't anything really weird and magical about herbs anyway; after all, aspirin came from willow, didn't it? And wasn't there something about foxgloves and heart attacks?

The book was in alphabetical order; bloodroot, borage, butter snakeroot, cross-wort, cuckoo pint, datura, dragon's blood, ergot, eye-bright … Surely she didn't expect me to learn about all of these? Fenugreek, fever bush … feverfew. At last. At the place where I opened the book was a folded sheet of paper. I opened it. There was a column of dates, starting about ten years ago. As I read what was listed, I went cold.

'Jan: Dog dirt through letterbox.
March: Tree cut down across drive.
June: 3 phone calls, silent.
July: Phone call, breathing.
August: Strawberries taken.'

I scanned down the list; spiders through the letter box, the tail feathers of her black cockerel cut off, a grass snake in the kitchen, red paint spilled on her driveway, more phone calls, something called a 'hex' made with string and feathers. And dead chicks. Lots of them. My head swam. I turned over the page to see the list continue. A small black-and-white photo of Annie, taken from a distance, had been stapled to the back of the paper. Annie's face had been scratched out.

I stuffed the paper back into the pages, and slammed the book shut with a puff of old dust. It was much worse than she'd let on. These village boys Annie had talked about, they might have been boys when they started their nasty pranks, but they'd be grown men by now. Either that or they'd recruited more boys to keep up the pressure. Why? Could it really just be because they thought she was a witch? Did they really think she had the power to raise storms or curse cattle, or whatever old-fashioned witches were meant to have done? A shiver ran down my spine as another thought occurred to me. Maybe the pranks were a distraction from the real issue; she'd said she guarded the hill. What if this wasn't about Annie at all, but a way to scare her off so they could get to the hill and whatever weird power it had?

No. How ridiculous. I was not going to get drawn into any supernatural nonsense. I pushed the book back into the shelf and pulled myself together. Think rationally. It was probably just a bunch of bored boys teasing an old woman. Little gits. If I ever found out who they were … No wonder she'd shouted at me when she first saw me on the hill.

Annie was out seeing to the goats and her kitchen was quiet. The afternoon sun and the heat from the Aga made the room cosy, and the dogs, especially old Noggin, were snoring. A word came into my head: becalmed. It was almost as if the cottage was paying close, loving attention to me. It was so quiet I had to give a little cough, just to make sure I hadn't gone deaf. A photo of a woman in a frock, who must have been Annie's mother, stood on the mantlepiece. She didn't look like a witch, any more than Annie did. Next to it a young Annie held her husband's arm on their wedding day. A shaft of afternoon sun passing through the coloured bottles on the sill sent rainbows across the walls. Tiny specks of dust sailed in the bright light. Nell looked up and sneezed. Then suddenly she turned to the door and growled softly. I looked up with a start.

A man stood in the doorway. He was tall with ruddy cheeks and he wore the check shirt and waxed jacket of a farmer. His dog, slinking around his ankles, had the same bright stare as him, though the collie's eyes were yellow and his were a washed-out blue.

"Gave you a shock, did I?" He laughed. "Sorry about that. You must be Olivia," he said, touching his cap. "She told me how you dropped in on her at the weekend. I'm Jack Denham. Manage the farm down at Lower Gillett. Pleased to meet you."

"You too," I muttered, but inside I was panicking. He seemed friendly enough, but I didn't want Mum knowing I was here.

"I reckon, apart from you, I'm Annie's only visitor up here. I brought her a few groceries." He smiled, waving a plastic bag. "Not that she needs much, what with all her goats and hens 'n' what not. Don't even need sugar in her tea what with those bees."

"Will you come in?" I muttered, hoping he'd say no.

"No. I won't stay. Gotta get on."

He handed me the bag and gestured up to the cottage roof.

"Shame to see this place falling apart, innit? I been up there a few times to try to patch it up but there's wet rot up there. Reckon it could cave in any day. I keep telling her she should get herself one o' those nice little sheltered accommodation places on the seafront and have done with all the work, but she won't hear none of it. And you don't mess with Annie Tilke, not if you know what's good for you. Well, you know what they say in the village about her?"

He narrowed his eyes and I frowned, not knowing how to answer. Then he laughed, a big, too-loud laugh, an indoors, pub laugh.

"If you could see your face. Listen, Annie was my old mum's best friend; I known her all my life. I reckon since you're here, you already know better than to listen to village gossip."

I smiled weakly.

He whistled his dog close and she slunk obediently to him. Then he set off out the door, calling, "Nice to meet you," after him.

"Oh, was Jack here? You should have called me." said Annie when she got back.

"Nell, you stupid dog, come here and be nice."

Nell crawled over to her on her belly.

"She don't like Jack's dog Trixie. Oh, but he's a good boy, Jack. He looks after me. His mother was always hard on him, said he wasn't a worker, but he's proved her wrong. Don't know how he finds time to go into town to get me bits and bobs."

"He says your roof's got wet rot."

"He's been saying that for years. Hasn't come to much so far. He's a good boy. He worries about me." A sudden thought came to her. "Don't you go saying nothing to him about what those village boys done. I don't want to trouble him."

"I still think you should tell the police about your greenhouse," I muttered. "Not all police officers are useless. My dad would have sorted it out for you."

She waved the idea away. "D'you know, a couple of years ago, Mr Jenkins – Oliver Jenkins, what owns the farm Jack manages, Lower Gillett – offered to buy the top fields off me. I reckon it was Jack who put him up to it. Trying to help me out, money-wise."

"The hill? You didn't agree, did you?"

"Course not. Rowan Hill ain't for sale. You know why. I told him I'd muddle through, somehow. It was a nice thought, though."

"Yeah, I suppose."

"So you'll come back tomorrow, will you?"

"If I can. After school, while it's still light in the evenings. And weekends." I hesitated. "Annie, the country stuff, I mean the plants and the animals, I really want to learn it. But the rest of it, the spells and charms … I'm just not into it. Alright?"

She said nothing, but smiled knowingly, reached out and patted my hand with her papery fingertips.

As I was leaving, she turned to me. "Best not let anyone see you coming here, and don't say nothing." She sounded casual but I could tell she was nervous. "Jack's alright, but some of them others …"

"I'll be careful," I promised.

9 – With a Fool No Seasons Spend

Every weekday the school bus pulled up right outside my door. There were upsides and downsides to travelling by bus. Richard Waddington, aka Wadsy, was proving a big downside.

"Oi, Livster, what's the matter? Time of the month? Got the painters in?" Wadsy thought he was being funny.

I blushed and slid into my seat near the back of the bus. Only Sadie knew my secret; I was the only girl in our year that hadn't started her periods yet. Wadsy didn't care. Whatever came into his head came out of his mouth. He didn't care if it was stupid or hurt your feelings. He was just like some out-of-control dog that knocked over people's precious vases with its tail and never even noticed.

"Wooo! I reckon she *must* have got her blob on. Look at the face on her. She don't want to talk to us no more, Rob. Women, huh?"

Robert Enticott, the upside of my daily bus ride, just shrugged himself deeper into his coat and closed his beautiful long eyelashes. Not one to take a hint, Wadsy went and sat next to him, and drummed on the empty seat next to me. He was always licking those thin lips of his. He smelt bad, stale boy-smells of cigarettes and sweat.

"My dad's kicking me out after exams so I'm going to live with my brother in Exeter. Gonna have the best time. Gonna go out down the quay every night and get wrecked."

"Gotta bed for me, too, has he, Wadsy?" Robert Enticott had opened one eye. "My dad's proper winding me up at the moment. Maybe I'll come and live with you and Trev."

Robert was still brown from a summer working outdoors. The way my stomach lurched when I was near him made me cross and confused. The only time he had ever spoken to me was to ask to copy my maths homework.

"That'd be brilliant." said Wadsy. "I'll ask him. Imagine us living in Exeter. How much fun would we have? But I don't want to be there when you break that one to your dad, Robsy. Ain't you taking over the farm any day now? I thought that was the plan."

"Taking over the farm? That's a laugh. He doesn't trust me to muck out the cattle shed, let alone run his precious farm. From the way he goes on, you'd think he'd be glad to retire and see the back of it." He put on his dad's broad Devon accent. "Can't get no money for milk since the supermarkets tied everything up. Might as well pour it down the drain. Vet's bills are something else." Robert scowled. "Drives himself mad jealous looking at the big farms. I told him there's no point comparing, that he should be happy with what he's got, but he don't listen to a bloody word I say. You heard his latest? Got his heart set on a new tractor."

"Bloody hell, that'll set him back a bob or two."

"Yeah. What's wrong with the old one, I don't know."

I'd never heard Robert say so much. His dark eyebrows were bunched together and his hands made fists in his lap. Suddenly he looked my way. For a second our eyes met. I looked away quickly so he didn't think I was being nosy, or, worse still, pitying him.

"He reckons the reason the farm doesn't make money is 'cos it's not productive enough," he went on. "I reckon it's 'cos he spends all the money on bloody gadgets. If he doesn't get off my back and start giving me a say in how it's run, I reckon I'm going to jack it all in."

Wadsy was wide eyed. "But the farm's been going forever, Robsy. I hope you got the key to the shotgun cupboard when you tell your old man. Yeah, I don't wanna be there when you tell him you're getting out of farming. Wait – you're having me on, ain't you?" he asked hopefully. Wadsy couldn't handle anything being serious for long. He poked Robert in the ribs until he got a reaction.

Robert cuffed him round the head.

"I *knew* you was having me on. Robsy, mate. Eh, Liv, you gonna come and visit me in Exeter?"

'As if,' I thought.

We arrived at school. There was a crush to get off the bus. Suddenly Robert was close behind me, his breath in my ear. "Saw you in the lane leaving Annie Tilke's house at the weekend. You sure your little old lady's as sweet as she looks?"

For a second my brain stopped working. His closeness was so intimidating, and yet I knew I'd want to remember and replay every second of it later. The bus was too crowded to step forward and away from him. All I could do was squeak, "She's alright", as the doors opened and I scurried off the bus.

"Yeah? Just you be careful not to cross her," he called after me in a mocking voice.

Bastard. He'd enjoyed making me squirm. That was the only reason he'd pressed up against me. And to think just a moment before, I'd felt sorry for him. I cursed myself, both that he'd seen me at Annie's, and that I hadn't come up with a wittier answer.

)X(

There were some rusty swings on the playing fields behind the sports hall. Now we were in Year Eleven it was okay to play at being kids again, because we knew we weren't. I loved kicking my feet high and feeling the lurch as the swing dragged me back. It sucked out the worries about Annie, exams, about Dad. Sadie's hair was a mad tangle as she heaved herself higher and higher to keep up with me.

"What are you going to do for your work experience?" I shouted.

Like Mr Dory had said, after Christmas we were all meant to do a placement somewhere, to get us out in the real world.

"I reckon I'll try to spend a couple of weeks at my old primary school," she shouted back. "Good practice for teacher training college. You?"

"I don't know. Mum wants me to do it in an office."

"What?" Sadie hooted, laughing so hard it made the swing wobble. "I can't see that working. Haven't you told her yet? What you really want to do?"

"No. But I know she wouldn't let me work on a farm. She'd think it was ridiculous."

"What a bitch."

"You can't say that about Mum!" I snorted.

"Yes, I can. Bitch, bitch, BEEE-YATCH. You say it. It feels *goood*."

"I can't say it."

"Yeah, you can. Better out than in, my dad would say."

I shook my head. "She's not a bitch, not really. It's just, you know, with my dad and everything. It's complicated."

Sadie's parents sounded like proper hippies; her dad was a therapist, the kind of person my dad gave a wide berth to. He certainly wasn't into this 'better out than in' theory. He never ever talked about his accident. Sadie's mum was some sort of artist.

"But your mum's meant to encourage you, not put limits on you," continued Sadie. "Being a vet's a brilliant ambition. After all, you're a country person now, aren't you?"

It wasn't true, but I loved her for saying it. Her parents were townies, but she had been born here. It made a big difference.

"Listen, you're not planning on going back to London any time soon, are you?" she asked anxiously.

"I really hope not. We only just got here. Mum hates it here though."

"Liv, whatever your mum says, you can't work in an office. You'd go mad."

"I know. But she just doesn't get it. After all, *she'd* love to be in an office."

"Well, good for her. You might be her daughter but you're not her clone."

We heard the bell go and hurriedly scuffed our swings to a standstill. Sadie checked her make-up in her pocket mirror and I watched her pull herself upright, ready to confront anyone who challenged her. Sadie always spoke her mind. It got her into trouble, but she didn't let that stop her. If only I was brave like her.

"I dunno. Maybe Mum's right. This vet thing. Perhaps I am being silly. We might not be in the countryside forever," I muttered.

"Oh, forever. That's ages away. Come on, Liv. They won't believe in you until you believe in yourself. You can't let things just *happen* to you. You've got to make them happen."

10 – Keep Unwelcome Spirits Out

Last lesson of the day was double biology. We were doing a dissection.

"Right, class. The moment you have all been waiting for. I have enough eyeballs for one between two. Wait for instructions. That means you, Mr Waddington."

Sadie squeezed my arm. She and her family were all vegetarians and she wasn't looking forward to the dissection. Wadsy, on the other hand, was almost drooling with excitement. He could hardly keep on his stool. He was so predictable. It was just a case of waiting for him to do the obvious. He had paired himself with Robert Enticott, who sat slouched against the wall. Wadsy dug him in the ribs and Robert retaliated with an angry shove.

"Get off, Wadsy. I'm not in the mood," he growled.

"That's enough," reprimanded Mr Dory, picking up the tray of eyeballs. As he neared our desk I felt nervous. I had to have the stomach for this.

"It's huge." Sadie said as he used tongs to place it on our dissection tray. The eye was about the size of a child's fist. It stared at us from inside a ball of pinkish fat and muscle. I stared back at it. Until yesterday, this eye was alive, I thought.

"Right, class. I would like you to pick up your eyeballs and notice the four sets of muscles that work on a cow's eyes. Unlike us, the cow can only look up, down, and side to side. That's why cows have to move their heads to get full vision."

I picked up the eye. It was heavy. I was beginning to get a sense of how it felt to be a cow. Behind the eye I imagined the animal, right there in the science lab. The cows that had been attached to the eyeballs shuffled and lowed, splattering the lab with their dung. I pulled the muscles about the eye and it bulged with the bug-eyed look of a terrified animal. I hoped it wasn't too scared when they killed it. I released the muscles and the eye went flaccid and wrinkled like the dead thing it was.

"Still want to be a vet, Liv?" Sadie nudged me, her brown eyes twinkling.

"Oh, Sadie, I wish I could spend my whole life surrounded by animals, learning to understand them, to protect them." I felt suddenly shy. "Does that sound stupid?"

"It's me you're talking to, not your mum. You're brilliant at science. You said yourself, you love animals and they love you. Your friend Annie even said you had a way with them, didn't she? You'll make a brilliant vet." My friend grinned.

"Olivia," a voice said sharply in my ear. I jerked up my head.

"Sir?" I answered automatically.

Mr Dory looked up at me from his desk on the other side of the room. "Yes, Olivia?" he asked.

"You … you said my name," I replied but even as I said it, I doubted myself. Behind the metallic smell of the blood from the dissection there was something else: the sharp smell of rotting leaves, dank earth and mildew.

"No, I didn't," he replied.

Bruised grass, crushed berries, the acid sap of roots. A round of giggles told me no one else had heard the voice either.

"Sadie, can you smell something?" I stammered. Cold waves of fear and confusion swept went through me. 'It's the smell of the blood, it must be doing funny things to me,' I told myself. 'Making me imagine things. Either that or I'm going mad, what's it called when you hear voices, schizophrenia, is it? Maybe the stress of Dad's accident, the move. Maybe I am losing my mind, perhaps I should get some fresh air.'

"Olivia."

My name. Again. I hadn't imagined that. For a second the hubbub of the classroom faded away and I was back on the hill, with the storm surging round me. I felt light-headed; I stepped off my stool and dropped to a crouch, my head low to the floor. It was the same voice. A voice that somehow came from deep within Rowan Hill. Not a human voice, but the sound of the hill itself. Here and now and as urgent as before. I couldn't ignore it.

"Alright," I whispered. "I don't know what you are or why you keep speaking to me, but you've got my attention. Now what do you want?" There was no answer, only the sound of blood throbbing in my temples. Almost as soon as it had swelled, the storm began to ebb, and the roaring in my ears receded. I was back in the classroom. Sadie was kneeling down next to me, holding my elbow.

"Are you feeling alright, Olivia?" asked Mr Dory.

"Just felt a bit faint," I muttered, standing up. "I'm better now."

Sadie looked at me quizzically. I wondered if she'd heard me speaking. Quickly she patted my arm then decided to pull focus from my weird behaviour. "Sir, what happens to the other bits of the cow? Lips, eyelids, ears and stuff?" she asked.

"School dinners," shouted Wadsy.

"For once you are right, Richard. Salvaged meat does go into things like cheap beefburgers," my teacher replied. "Other than that, pet food, fertiliser or incineration, I suppose. Perhaps it's best not to think about, eh, Sadie?"

"With all due respect, sir," Sadie retorted, sounding not in the least respectful, "That's a complete cop-out. We should think about where our food comes from, and the animal that died to give us our beefburger. Or don't you agree, sir?"

Mr Dory was briefly flummoxed. Then he chuckled, shaking his head. "Quite right, quite right, what would we do without you, Sadie? You are the moral conscience for the class. But shall we continue that discussion another time?"

Sadie graciously backed down; she had scored a point.

The smell of earth and vegetation had receded. I shivered, trying to shake the echo of the voice from my head. What had we been talking about when it spoke to me?

"Now, class, we are going to make an incision into the cornea. Cut carefully," instructed the teacher.

There was a shriek from across the lab. Becky Hunter's apron was splattered with brown liquid. Wadsy roared with laughter.

"That's the aqueous humour you've found there, Becky. It keeps the pressure in the eye."

"This is gross, sir," chimed in Wadsy. "It's brilliant!"

"Glad you are enjoying yourself, Richard. Okay, class. Please remove the top half of the cornea."

With a brown spurt, our eye deflated. Now it was just a ball of gore. My imaginary heifer faded away.

"Two minutes ago it was part of an animal, and now it just looks like meat."

"Lucky for the butchers, that," said Sadie, wrinkling her nose. "You alright now?"

"Yeah, I think the smell of the blood made me go a bit funny," I bluffed.

The voice had shaken me, but more than anything, it had shaken me awake. I was confused but utterly elated; if I put aside the niggling worry that I was going mad, I was left with the weird alternative that this voice, whatever it was, had found me out again. That it had some kind of message that was meant for me alone. The thrill I felt flickered between excitement and fear. There was no time to question it now though. I didn't want to miss a moment of the dissection.

The eye had become a brilliantly constructed machine that we were taking apart. We removed the black lump of flesh called the iris and found the cow's pupil within it.

Wadsy poked his finger through the pupil. "Hey, Robsy, d'you like my ring?" he guffawed.

Next we removed the vitreous humour, a clear jelly blob. Wadsy stuck a finger in that too, to make it squelch. No one laughed at him anymore, not that he noticed. Finally, we discovered the lens lying hidden in the eye like a pearl in an oyster. We took turns reading enlarged print with the lens as a magnifying glass.

Without warning, something gory sailed through the air and landed with a 'spletch' on the wooden bench in front of us, smearing the bits of our own dissection across the table.

"Wadsy!" Sadie shouted.

"Waddington," roared Mr Dory, steaming towards the location of the missile.

"Me, sir? I never done nothing," Wadsy claimed, all innocence.

"Why do you always have to be so completely disrespectful," fumed my friend. The tip of her nose always went pink when she was angry or emotional.

"Waddington. See me later."

"Yes, sir, sorry sir. Sorry Liv. Sorry Sadie."

Sadie was livid with outrage. "Don't apologise to me, you idiot. You should be apologising to the cow."

After the class Mr Dory stopped me. "How are you feeling now, Olivia?"

"I'm fine," I reassured him. "It was just a bit hot in the classroom."

"Good. Can't have you fainting in dissections if you're going to be a vet, now, can we? Did you speak to your parents about doing some work experience yet?"

My heart sank. "Umm, not yet."

"Well do. The deadline is fast approaching. I wouldn't want to see you wasting a golden opportunity."

After he'd gone, I stood there, trying to get a grip on the dread and excitement that took turns to overwhelm me. There was no getting away from it; the conversation with Mum and Dad was really important. And the voice, why had I heard it now? It was all tied up together. If only I could work out how.

11 – Heed Ye Flower, Bush and Tree

"A month you been here, and already you think you can tell me what's what, do you?" Annie shouted, stamping down the corridor away from me. "I managed perfectly well before you came along, I'll have you know."

"But this time you've got to call the police. They can't keep doing this to you."

"You got a very high opinion of the police. Got that from your dad, I suppose. They won't do anything. Come up here, sniff about. Then accuse me of wasting their time."

"No, they wouldn't. This is theft.

"You're telling me. The whole bloody crop. Not a single plum left on a branch. The little toads. I could throttle 'em."

Every time I caught up with her, she marched out of the room into another one.

"How did they get up the lane without you hearing them? It must have taken ages to pick all that fruit," I shouted at her disappearing back.

"How am I meant to know?" she snapped. "All I know is, there'll be no plum chutney this year. No plum wine. No plum jam neither."

"Annie, you must call the police. It's not like it's the first time. I know this has been going on much longer than you've let on."

"How do you know?"

"There was a piece of paper, in the herb book—"

"Oh, spying on me now, are you? You keep your fingers out of my private letters."

"You're not just going to sit here and let them walk all over you, are you?"

She turned on her heel and fixed me with a withering look. "Of course not. Here, I made these." From the windowsill she took down one of the bottles, and I saw that she'd filled it with lengths of coloured thread. Other bottles glinted with broken glass. "A fail-safe charm to keep intruders out." Annie sniffed with satisfaction at her work. "If ill will tries to enter this house, the string will tangle it, the glass will tell it that it can't pass. They'll protect me better than old PC Plod, in any case."

I was lost for words. It was almost too stupid to be true. "Tell me you're joking. You're joking right?"

"This ain't no joking matter."

"Exactly. Which is why you should stop being so totally ridiculous and call the police."

"No."

"Well then if you won't, I will."

"You do that and you'll never set foot in my house again. Got it?"

Two hours later we were still barely speaking but a warm, wonderful smell filled the house. The damp from the leaky roof had made Annie's chest bad and she was making a cough syrup from a recipe in her mother's book.

"Right, I need hyssop, liquorice root, aniseed and elecampane root," she said.

"What was the last one you wanted? Ele … what?"

"Elecampane. It's in the big jar on the top shelf, next to the angelica. Bring some of that in too. I can't leave this or it'll burn." She stirred some of her precious honey on the stove, skimming off the scum as it boiled.

In the still room I scanned across the labels looking for elecampane. There was Annie's mother's faded copperplate, here Annie's newer, blacker italics, and on just a few jars of herbs I'd helped gather with Annie in the last weeks, my own clear, round hand. 'Hemp Agrimony'. 'Meadow Sweet'. 'Burdock'. Those labels made me uncomfortable, like I had somehow signed my agreement to become the next generation's witch. I unstoppered the jar containing hyssop and inhaled the minty smell of the dried leaves before fetching down the rest of the herbs.

In Annie's book there were remedies for all sorts of illnesses, recipes for teas, perfumes, incense. But no one ever came to be treated. A large jar of shrivelled toadstools on the top shelf caught my eye; the label read 'Fly Agaric'. Next to it stood belladonna, henbane and hemlock – the poisons.

Annie was at the door. I wasn't sure how long she had been watching me. "Don't get ahead of yourself," she cautioned me coldly. "In the wrong hands, even healing herbs can kill. You've got a lot to learn."

While the mixture was cooling, we went for a walk. Whether I wanted it or not, every time I saw her, she filled me with lessons. And on a good day her teaching made the hedges, hills and trees come into sharper focus; the countryside was bigger, deeper, more mine. I felt my feet embedding themselves more firmly in the soil and I could almost feel myself taking root. But today I was frustrated; our row had unsettled me.

I looked ruefully towards the hilltop; the walls of the house were just visible behind the screen of rowans. Annie had kept her word and refused to speak to me about the voice, and since the day of the dissection it had stayed silent. As time went on, the more convinced I was that I hadn't imagined it. A craving had begun to grow. Just a whisper. Please. Something to make sense of things. Something that would explain what all this stuff Annie was teaching me was for.

"What's this flower called?" Annie demanded, jerking me out of my private thoughts.

"Uh, vetch?"

"Come on, Livvy. Stop your daydreaming. It's yarrow. Good for infections. I showed you in the book, remember?"

"Okay. I'm doing my best. There's just so much to learn. It's alright for you. You grew up here. You've known this stuff for years."

"What of it? You've got a young brain, if only you'd apply some of it …"

"I just don't see how learning about a bunch of flowers is going to help me understand what happened on the hill," I muttered.

"I thought you were interested in herb lore. You think naming things is all about owning them. 'Tisn't that at all. Naming helps you see things better. Appreciate them better."

"I am interested. But what's it got to do with anything? You expect me to learn it but you don't tell me what for."

"You've got to understand how things connect. How to keep the balance."

"What do you mean? That's just gobbledegook."

"Look, it wasn't me that chose you for a student," she retorted. "I might've chosen someone who could speak civil to their teacher."

The cold light in her eyes should have made me bring the conversation to an end, but her stubbornness about the vandalism was driving me crazy.

"Look, Annie, I'm grateful, I am. But do you really think a bunch of string in a bottle is going to keep those boys away, if that's what they are?"

"Oh, this again."

"What if they hurt you? Or your animals? It's stupid."

"Not to my way of thinking." She sniffed. "Not to others neither. You might put no faith in charms, but time was, people came from all over this valley to me for help. In love, in sickness, to mend their fortunes."

"But they don't come anymore, do they?" I said spitefully.

She turned to me angrily. "No, they don't. Maybe you want to go and ask those gossips in the village why? Then perhaps you won't want to come no more neither."

And with that she stood and stomped off down the hill.

"NO, NO, NO!"

I was still sulking in the field when I heard her cries and started running. I found her at the back of the barn where the bee hives stood. The white wooden lids were off, and each one was empty but for a husk of dried-up comb and a few dead bees in the bottom. I helped her to a nearby log where she sat in a crumpled heap, wringing her hands with worry.

"Liv, I never known 'em leave before. It's a bad sign. Oh, you mark me, it's a terrible sign."

I searched each hive again. Not a single living bee remained.

"Did the village boys do this?" I demanded.

"No, no, I don't think they could make 'em leave."

"Then what's made them go?"

Wearily she put her head in her hands. "There's only two things that make bees leave. The first is swarming. It ain't that, 'cos none of 'em stayed behind. Here, hand me one of them combs."

I pulled out a wooden slat. It contained the remains of the honey comb, heavy with the pulpy white bodies of hundreds of dead bee larva.

"That settles it. They left their young to die. The colony must've been in real trouble. They've not swarmed, they've deserted."

"But why would they do that?"

"I dunno. Bees are a mystery. No one understands bees, not really. Least of all how much we need 'em."

I squatted down next to her. "I saw this programme about a place in China where they've got thousands of men with little paintbrushes pollinating all the trees and plants, because the bees have all gone," I said. "On the programme they said a mite was killing them off, making them too weak to get back to the hive. Either that or it was pesticide." I was glad to have some kind of rational explanation to offer.

She nodded bleakly. "Look at the hillside yonder. What colour is it?"

"Green."

"Exactly. Plain, flat green. Nothing but grass and not a wild flower in sight 'cause they're not so useful to farmers, your foxgloves, your comfrey, your vetch, are they? Gotta grow richer grass for the cows so they use herbicides and more fertilisers. More grass, more milk, more beef. More, more, more. When will we realise that there's limits?" Annie reached for my hand and gripped it hard. "Oh, Liv, Nature's crying out. We've pushed her too hard, asked too much of her. Now it's us that will pay the price."

12 – Go by Waxing Moon

A few days later, Sadie and I were back on the swings. It was a beautiful day, and we were trying to forget our troubles by flinging ourselves into the blue.

Sadie kicked off her shoes; they flew in an arc, sailing over the high hedge that separated the swings from the playing field.

"Oi! Bloody hell!" someone shouted.

"Knickers," hissed Sadie, slowing her swing down. "Sorry," she called, before trotting off in her socks to apologise.

I skidded myself to a stop and waited for her. After a few minutes I peeked round the hedge to see what she was up to.

Sadie was chatting with a couple of boys. She was standing with her weight on one leg, running her hand through her hair and laughing. "Look who I nearly took out with my shoes. That was to get you back for the cow's eye, Waddington."

Wadsy, who for some reason was wearing a knackered-looking leather biker's jacket over his school uniform, jumped up, fag in hand, when he saw me. "Alright Liv? Didn't think we'd see you over here on the playing fields. Having a crafty smoke, was you? I reckon it's always the good girls you gotta watch out for."

He was gabbling again, and I can't say that I really paid him much attention, because on the bench, hunched over and looking down at his feet, was Robert Enticott. He didn't look up; he was busy striking match after match, burning them down to his bitten fingertips and letting them fall. I noticed how calloused his hands were; his bitten fingernails were chipped and stained, the ends of his fingers engrained with dirt from oily machinery.

Sadie seemed excited, and it was clear she wanted to stay and chat. We were only two minutes from school grounds, but this was new territory. Things felt unpredictable. "Where are you going to do your work experience, Robert?" she said, sitting down on the bench next to him.

He guffawed. "What's the point in me doing work experience? I'm on permanent bloody work experience as it is. And I can't see me getting a promotion in a hurry neither. Not planning on coming back for A levels anyway. Waste of time for the likes of me."

Sadie looked crestfallen. "Oh, that's a shame."

"Hey, maybe I should get Dad to write me a report. I know what it'd say though. Could do better." He wasn't making it easy for her.

"Cheer up, Rob," Wadsy pleaded. "These lovely ladies don't wanna hear you moaning on. Look, you're gonna scare Liv off in a minute. We ain't gonna bite you, Liv."

I ducked behind my hair and gave Sadie a 'let's go' look. She ignored me. She was examining Wadsy's cigarette packet. I thought for a minute she was going to light up, to try to impress them, but instead she studied the picture of the man with throat cancer, grimacing.

"Gross," she said.

Wadsy changed the subject. "You girls up for any of the Young Farmers' nights then? No, don't be like that. They're a right laugh. Don't tell me you ain't been before? They have 'em in one of the village halls but they got a sound system and lights and everything, an' a bar, that's the main thing. I'm a bloody brilliant dancer, I am, ain't I, Rob?" Wadsy was performing now, in his element. "That last one, down Axford, I got so wrecked I slept in a ditch after."

Despite myself, I laughed. Wadsy was a clown. Robert looked up in surprise when he heard me and almost smiled himself. This made Wadsy beam; if he were a dog, he'd have licked us with gratitude.

"If the music's crap we all go out and sit by the river drinking, or go up the hill fort," he grinned. "It's not just farmers, girls, not that there's anything wrong with farmers." He made faces at the top of Robert's head for our benefit. "Lots of townies come in too. Last year, Robsy here got in a fight with this bloke from Taunton, you should have seen it kick off. We chased him down the road and I heard he got so lost in the back lanes he'd walked halfway back to Taunton before his mates found him. Bloody brilliant it was!"

It was Sadie's turn to laugh now. "Well, you've almost tempted me," she said sarcastically. "How about you, Olivia?"

"Aw, go on, Liv, come out with us? What else you got on, anyhow?" Wadsy begged.

Robert stood up and chucked his matchbox in the bin. His voice was unexpectedly mean. "Don't pester her, Wadsy. Liv's busy. Busy up at Annie Tilke's mostly, ain't you?"

I froze, but he went on.

"All very well you helping out with her animals, but I gotta tell you, you ain't making no friends in the village, Liv."

In defence of Annie I found my voice. "Who says I want friends in the village?"

Robert shook his head, full of false concern. "Well, I don't know how you stomach it."

"Oh, for God's sake!" I retorted. "You're pathetic, you and the rest of your village."

"Come on, Liv," declared Sadie, taking my arm and marching me away.

"Annie Tilke, ain't she the one who ...?" We left Wadsy pawing Robert for answers.

"What was all that about?" Sadie wanted to know.

"Just ignorant people being cruel about an old woman."

"You mean Annie? Your old lady with the animals? What was he on about, 'I don't know how you stomach it'?" she asked, putting on Robert's deep Devonian voice.

I took a deep breath and decided to come clean with Sadie about Annie's bullies. "It's so stupid. Annie collects herbs and stuff. Makes little charms. So they call her a witch."

"Cool." replied Sadie with shining eyes.

"Well, not cool for her. For years now nasty stuff has been happening to her because of it. Dog poo through her letterbox. They smashed up her greenhouse. I don't know what to do."

"Why didn't you tell me?" Sadie demanded looking hurt.

"Sorry. It's just she's so secretive about it. She won't go to the police. She gets angry if I talk about it. I've been trying to figure out what to do."

"But who's doing it? Who would want to do that to her?"

"I don't know. There's some sort of village gossip that Wadsy and Robert seem to know about but I'm not giving them the satisfaction of asking them. And anyway, how do I know it's not them who are the vandals? Robert's been in trouble with the police loads of times."

"Well, why don't you lie in wait, catch them at it. Take photos or something?" Sadie began excitedly.

"I thought of that, but I've no way of knowing when they might come. I can't wait every night. And what if they're dangerous?" I trailed off.

Sadie scoffed and turned away, disappointed by her unadventurous friend.

I changed the subject. "What is it with you and Robert anyway?" I bluffed. "You total tart."

"Was I that obvious?" Sadie giggled.

"Yes." I confirmed.

"Oh, I'm only human, Liv. God, talk about tall, dark and handsome."

"Tall, dark and miserable, more like," I replied, but she was off, swooning and twirling across the grass.

"Aww, come on, he's gorgeous. Did you see his eyes? They're so brown they're almost black. I can't believe he's only our age. He looks like he's nearly twenty. Anyway, miserable is what makes him interesting. He's complicated."

"I thought you said he was just a grumpy git?" I reminded her, but she waved me away.

"I tell you. Hidden depths, that's what he's got. Not like Wadsy. Now he is obvious. The way he looks at you."

I didn't like where this was going. "What do you mean?"

"He fancies the pants off you, Liv, can't you tell?"

"Nooo." I hid my head in my hands and moaned.

"What did he say? 'Aw, go on, Liv, come out with us?'" she mimicked. "Well, you are gorgeous."

"Yeah, right," I joked. I didn't feel gorgeous. Especially around Robert Enticott. He made me feel clumsy and ugly.

"You are! You're a total goddess. Much too good for Wadsy. But we are so going to Young Farmers. Don't worry, I'll protect you."

"But who's going to protect Robert from you?" I joked.

She pretended to be scandalised before blowing me a big kiss.

☽○☾

"I'm not interested in gossip, Wadsy," I told him as we got on the school bus, before he had a chance to start on again about Annie. It was a lie. I was interested in gossip. I had to be because it might help me work out who was bullying her and if it was tied up with her guarding the hill. I just couldn't bear to hear any more of their cruelty. I sat at the front of the bus so Wadsy would leave me alone.

"But you know what they say about her, Liv? I only—"

"Leave her, Wadsy," Robert cut him off as he boarded the bus. "What she don't know won't kill her."

I didn't like the way Wadsy laughed as Robert pushed him to their usual seats at the back of the bus.

13 – True in Love

"Dogs need a walk," said Annie when we'd finished our chores for the day. "Come on. It'll take my mind off the bees."

The cows in the low field stumbled to their feet as the dogs trotted close to the gate. They were young and curious, with folds of flesh at their necks that trembled as they stretched out beaded noses to snuff and huff for our scent. They rolled their eyes at the dogs, balking and starting back, until the braver ones inched forwards. I thought of the eye I had dissected and felt uncomfortable.

"Look at them flies. I shall have to douse 'em with mugwort. I got some dried, somewhere. Oh, it's torture, me dears," commiserated Annie.

While she was talking to the cows, I climbed the hill. Behind me I could feel the view tempting me to turn, but I kept going. This was my game with myself. How high could I climb before claiming my reward? Today I would get to the top. I ran hard to the summit before turning and drinking it in.

The sun on the slopes caught the contours of the land, and the trees and hedgerows cast long shadows. Annie had told me that the tall hedgerows were planted hundreds of years ago for penning in stock, that the fields of deep green grass were those given over to grazing, whereas those yellowed and cut already were for winter fodder, to be fermented down into silage. Even the fertile air told you that cattle were kept here. A rich-smelling breeze made the grass on Annie's hill ripple. The valley fell away below me before rising up into a steep woodland of young oaks. Beyond it, the hills rolled away into the far distance, taking my heart with them until they evaporated into a glimpse of sea and an expanse of blue sky.

Annie caught up with me and laughed. Hand on hip, she paused to catch her breath.

"When I look at this view, I think my chest's going to explode," I told her, never taking my eyes from it. "It's the most beautiful thing I've ever seen." I wanted so much to belong here.

Annie linked her arm through mine, and I squeezed it tight. She smiled. "Sounds like you're in love, girl."

Perhaps this was what love felt like. Like your soul was expanding and melding into the thing you loved.

Annie went on, "It's paradise, isn't it? They talk about heaven waiting for us when we die. I reckon it's already here, if you have the eyes to see it."

As we walked closer to the ruins of Rowan House, I began to feel something. The kind of expectant stillness I'd felt on the day of the storm and again in the classroom. I fought back my fear and excitement. It was better to expect nothing than be disappointed. And yet, this was different. The air was charged, as if something knew we were coming. We stopped by the circle of flickering rowans, their branches laden with bunches of orange berries. Annie placed her hand on a slim grey trunk and was silent for a few moments.

"Annie, tell me again—"

"I told you," she replied tersely. "We been through this, Liv. Whatever you saw, whatever you heard, it's for you to fathom your answers to." She looked up into the high branches of the rowan. "Some folks call them witness trees, because they've seen so much," Annie murmured. "Other folks call them the whispering trees. Ask them a question and maybe the answer will come, though maybe not how you expect it. You listening?" Quickly she turned on her heel and set off down the hill with Pip in her wake.

I continued on with Nell. Three crumbling walls: soon all that would be left would be a clearing and some piles of bramble-covered rubble. I put out my hand to touch the wall and my skin prickled with electricity; every stone, every leaf throbbed with meaning. What if there were things that you couldn't explain? Things far bigger and more mysterious than my books could prepare me for? My ears strained to hear a message from the trees but only white noise roared back. I leant my back against a wall. Nell was still snuffling in the undergrowth. She closed her mouth around something and brought her treasure to me.

"Drop it, that's it. Good girl, Nell," I told her. Into my hand she laid the withered body of a chick. Then she bounded back down the hill leaving me alone. I slid down to the ground. Trembling, I held the chick in both hands; it had hardly any weight at all.

I squeezed my eyes shut. "Who's hurting Annie?" I asked, and waited. Through my eyelids, dappled light flickered. Without sight, my other senses grew keen, reaching out for signals. I felt the day's heat radiating out of the earth and smelt pine needles. The crack of a seed case drying in the sun, the hum of an insect. Then a subtle movement that made my heart beat faster. A slight change in pressure, as if a door had opened or closed. The hairs on my neck rose. I felt something coming silently up the hill. I held my breath as it passed through the rowans, sweeping across the grass. A sweet, powerful energy seemed to pulse through the earth as it came; it seeped into the stones, it was sucked up by the roots of the trees and rose like sap to the highest branches. It flooded into me; I thought of green growing things. With it came the scent of apple blossom, fresh grass and warm earth.

I didn't dare open my eyes. The force of it pinned me up against the wall. I dropped the chick and spread out my fingers, feeling the power of the stones flood through me. My logic was all gone. It was as disinterested as Nature, neither good nor evil. But it was painfully beautiful and utterly terrifying. It searched me out, seeping through my blood. There was nothing I could hide from it; it saw me, it knew me. I understood how a rose feels when it opens for the life-giving, withering sun. It was so strong I thought it would destroy me, but then I felt a change; for all its strength it was as vulnerable as a new chick, as fragile as a rose. And it was fearful. It needed help. I reached out my arms to hold it to me, but almost as soon as it had come, I felt it moving away.

'Stay,' I begged silently. I couldn't bear to lose such fierce beauty so soon. I knew now why Annie craved it so much. But it was already ebbing away.

'*Olivia*,' breathed the voice.

"I don't understand. What do you want me to do?" I called to the deserted hilltop.

Pale remnants of a powerful energy flickered through the stones. Even though I couldn't explain it and had no name for it, I felt bolder, more alive for having felt it. The whispering trees had once more kept their secrets; the chick lay where I had dropped it, a silent recrimination. This was a mystery I knew I had to solve.

14 – Chanting Out the Wiccan Runes

The bright skies of early autumn were gone. Fat grey rain clouds had moved in and we'd had to hurry to get Annie's harvest in. There might have been no plums this year, but Annie's larder shelves now groaned with jars of rowan jelly, blackberry jam and bottles of rose hip cordial. Demijohns of dandelion and damson wine blipped quietly on the flagstones. Downstairs all was organised, but upstairs the damp had started to creep in; the white-washed plaster had come away from the wall in places to reveal the centuries-old wooden lattice stuffed with Red Devon cow hair.

The only warm room in the house now was the living room, near the fire. The dogs snored in piles next to us and we were both covered in dog hair. Annie had nodded off in her armchair. Her strong jaw sagged and her mouth hung open, tightening her white skin, making her face gaunt. I shook off a horrible premonition. But for the rattle of her chest as she breathed in, she could be dead. The honey cough mixture I'd helped her make, the day we had argued, was nearly all gone and yet she seemed no better. But she scoffed at the idea of going to a doctor. I knew she was scared they'd put her in a home. With a clack of her jaw, she was suddenly awake, moistening her dry mouth with her tongue and remembering where she was.

"Forty winks." She winked at me. Heaving herself up, she stoked the fire in the living room until it crackled. The walls ticked as the heat expanded them. I tried to relax, but the hard knots of worry in my chest and throat were back.

"How's your dad?" she asked, reading my mind.

"No better. It's like he's lost interest in life. Like he's lost hope."

Annie sucked the air between her teeth. "Ah, that's bad. Hope's the best medicine. You know there's healing charms I could work on him."

"Are there?" I asked. "What, like a herbal medicine?"

"No. Charms, Liv."

"Oh, right," I muttered. I wished she'd let it drop, this spells and magic stuff. Even though I had no explanations for the voice yet, still, I wasn't having any of it. It was embarrassing.

"He'd never agree to it." I imagined the scorn on Dad's face if I even suggested it. "I mean, it's not exactly logical, is it?"

"Belief's a funny thing. It doesn't always make sense, but that doesn't stop it being powerful," mused Annie, smiling at my crossness. "Oh well. Never mind then. How about you? You told 'em yet? That you're serious about becoming a vet? You've got to tell 'em sometime, Liv."

"It's not that easy," I said.

Annie shrugged. "I got something for you. Put your arm out." From her pocket she pulled out a length of red string and tied it round my wrist. She closed her eyes and I saw her lips moving.

"What's all that about then?" I laughed.

"A spell for courage." She smiled. "Oh, I know you don't believe a word of it, and I know you think I'm full of mumbo-jumbo. But it doesn't hurt to ask for help sometimes, does it?"

I pulled my sleeve down over the string. "It can't hurt I suppose," I admitted.

The fire crackled and a bright spurt of sparks flew up the chimney.

"Well, the fire says good news is coming, anyway." She laughed. She squeezed my hand in her gnarled one and heaved herself up to put another log on.

I crept in the back door of my house shortly after dark, with an invented story of where I had been all prepared. I needn't have worried. I could hear Mum upstairs on the phone, having one of her longed-for natter sessions with my sister Amber. I crept up to bed.

As I was about to drop off, just like he did every night, my dad started screaming.

15 – When the Moon Rides at Her Peak

Usually, it was Mum that got to him first, stumbling out from the separate bedroom she'd slept in since the accident. This time, she didn't wake and it was me that found him, sitting on the edge of his bed. His eyes were wild with panic. I wasn't sure he was fully conscious so I spoke to him like I'd heard Mum do, shushing him, reassuring him. He started away from me, not seeming to recognise me at first. But I put a hand on his shoulder. I heard his breathing grow calmer. Slowly I saw him return to himself.

After a few minutes he turned his head away. "I'm sorry, Olivia. You should go back to bed. No daughter should see their father like this."

"You should try to rest, Dad."

He looked exhausted. He glanced at the window. Through a crack in the curtains, I saw the moon hanging low and full in the sky. "The moon was full on the night of the accident," he said. "Did you know that? There are always more crimes when the moon is full. More nutters, more murders, more opportunists doing a bit of thieving. Ask any copper, he'll tell you that."

"Dad, please rest. You don't have to talk about it."

"Of course. You go back to bed. It's alright." He looked down at his feet. Everything about him looked so defeated, so alone, that I had to stay.

"Unless you want to," I added.

"They keep telling me I should talk. Get some help. The pills aren't working, Liv. I'm not getting better. I don't know if I will ever get better. Remembering what happened … talking about it … I …" He was already breathing fast. "Every bit of that night is printed on my memory, the colours, the sounds, the smells."

He looked up again then, but not at me. Up and out at the full moon; I could see he was already back there, on the night of the accident. "My beat took me down by the canal," he began. "At the start of the walk, there are willow trees, posh houses set back from the water's edge with high brick walls and burglar alarms. If you look in the dark windows round there you can see chandeliers and paintings. Then, as you walk on, you get to Victorian warehouses, all converted into swanky flats now. That night, there were people partying inside the flats; you could hear people smoking on the balconies, laughing."

I knew exactly the place he meant, though I'd never been there at night. As a kid, I had fed the ducks from that towpath. I'd always liked it, but Dad's accident had made it a sinister site.

"I kept walking, with Liz, the PC I shared the beat with. The brick work starts to crumble when you get past the lock, and these great big buddleia flowers grow out of it. They've got this strange smell at night-time, Liz said it was like purple velvet. We walked on past the big estates that give onto the canal, past the benches where the druggies and alkies hang out. We stopped to chat to a few of the blokes we knew. It was a warm night; the drunker ones didn't want to move on. They grumbled about it, but I always had a way of talking people round. I grew up round there and I know the lingo. They all thought I was a good bloke, so they shuffled off, trying to scab cigarettes on their way. I knew they'd settle down on another bench as soon as we left.

"The moonlight was weird; it made the water look silver, and ripples kept flashing against the bank every time a duck took off. Then, up ahead, we saw two figures. They had someone pushed up against the wall, but seeing us, they legged it. I set off running straight away, with Liz on the walkie-talkie back to the station.

"I shouted, 'Stop, police,' but they kept running, of course. The victim was on the ground. When I got to her, I quickly checked her over. She was bruised, her clothes were ripped, her bag had been nicked, but she was okay. She smelt of those disgusting alcopops I keep telling Amber to avoid, and her teeth were chattering. Liz caught up. 'Leave her with me. You go after them. I've called back-up,' she said. So I set off after the attackers. I was fit then. Thought I had a real chance of catching up with them."

Dad spoke in a low voice. He conjured the details so clearly I felt I was running after him along the towpath. "I remember, the noise of my feet sent the ducks flying off over the water. There was no sign of the muggers so I stopped. Up ahead there was a bend in the canal and a low bridge. The moonlight was reflected off the water and lit up the bridge's ceiling; it was bright enough to see right through it. I could see where, up ahead, the canal path gave off onto steps that would take the muggers away into streets, estates, onto buses. If they got away, we'd never find them.

"Then, at the bottom of the steps, I spotted someone catching their breath. 'Oi! You. Stop right there. Police!' I yelled and charged ahead. Course, I hadn't noticed the alcove in the wall under the bridge, or the mugger's mate hiding in it. And when I rushed in, the guy panicked and burst out of his hiding place, barging straight into me, pushing me hard in the chest. He caught me off guard. I couldn't breathe. It was a horrible moment. I thought he might have stabbed me."

Dad's eyes were wide and part of him seemed frozen, although his breathing was fast and ragged. "I flailed about for a second, trying to keep my balance but feeling my chest for blood. Then I fell backwards into the dark, stinking water." He was grim now, his eyes locked on his hands, which were twisting in his lap. "It was so dark in the water, Liv. I went down, under it. I still couldn't breathe. It closed over my head and everything went dark. I thought I'd had it. I thought, 'This is it, Pete.' And as I went down, I felt something touch my leg."

Now his left leg was juddering. It was horrible to watch. His voice had gone all little, like a boy's. "There was a car in the water, Liv, an old car. Rusting metal, shards of metal. I felt it as I went in. Half a metre to the left and I'd have lost an arm or a leg, they said. The darkness of the water. The shock of it. Liv. I thought I was going to die."

He roused himself out of the story. "It's pathetic, Liv. I've been a police officer most of my life, seen things, handled things, much, much worse than this. I fell into a canal. So what? I wasn't injured. It wasn't serious. I can't understand why it's shaken me up like this. It's pathetic. I'm pathetic."

"You're not, Dad. It's like the doctors said, you had a trauma. You might not have been badly hurt, but your brain still believed you were going to die."

I stretched out my hand to him. He pulled it away, mechanically.

"You'd best get back to your room," he instructed me.

Dumbly, I did as he asked while he pulled himself under his covers and reached over to switch off the light. His misery made him self-centred. He had no energy to care what effect the story might have on me. He didn't know, or didn't care anymore, how much we loved him.

Back in bed I lay looking at the ceiling. The silver moonlight leached the warmth from everything.

When he got home from hospital Dad wasn't the same, inside or out. He stopped sleeping for a start. Every night, just like tonight, Mum, me, Amber, we'd all lain awake, listening to his terrified dreams. He couldn't do police work anymore, and he was too ill and too proud to take the desk job they offered him. He had been walking the beat since he left school. He took his compensation and announced we were moving away from London, the scene of the crime.

The rest of that night Dad groaned for hours but I couldn't bear to go to him again. I squeezed the red string that wrapped my wrist, the charm my friend Annie had given me to give me courage. As dawn was breaking, Dad finally grew quieter, and I fell into a deep, dreamless sleep.

16 – Then the Heart's Desire Seek

Next morning, before going to breakfast, I touched the red band around my wrist then pulled down the sleeve of my shirt so my parents wouldn't see it.

"Please, Pete. Just try. It would be good for you to get out. The doctors say you need more company," Mum was saying as she washed the dishes.

"You go along and have a good time, Lisa. Leave me out of it. I don't need to be part of the village in-crowd," the top of Dad's head said into his newspaper.

"Well then, if you won't do it for you, do it for me." You had to hand it to her, she was persistent. "We'll never be accepted into this village if we don't start making a bit of effort. Come on, love, all the other women bring their husbands. The quiz teams are meant to have eight people in. The Dents are going, and the Lawsons, Sheila and Simon Staves are going, which leaves us a man down. Please come, Pete," she said in a hopeful voice.

"To make up the numbers? No thanks. I'm sure you'll find someone else." He lowered his paper, and his pale face and reddened eyes appeared over the top.

I shuddered to remember the story he'd told me the night before. I hated to think how often he relived it.

"Olivia, do you want something? Come in and shut the door. You're letting a draught in."

It was as if our conversation the previous night had never happened.

"It's about work experience ..." I began in my most confident voice. Then my confidence ebbed away and I trailed off.

"What is it, Liv?" Dad asked irritably. "What do you want?"

"I ... I want to be a vet," I blurted.

Mum stopped what she was doing and turned to face me with a look of astonishment. For a moment I saw the tiniest flash of pride in Dad's eyes. Then he looked down at his paper.

"Oh, that's a good one." he barked dryly. "D'you remember, Lisa, how we had to hide the *Bambi* video because looking at the box made her cry? Dream on, Liv. Maybe you need to set your sights a bit lower. I mean apart from that stray dog you picked up, which we had for, what, forty-eight hours, you've had hardly any dealings with animals. You've never even had a goldfish."

"I have to say, I agree with your father," Mum said, sounding relieved. "And, on top of that, it's a huge commitment. It takes years and years. Think of all the work. And ever so expensive. It's like I said to your sister, the sooner you get out to work, the sooner you can start standing on your own two feet. I left home at sixteen. And look at Amber, she's loving being a nanny," she added encouragingly.

Invisible hands were squeezing my throat shut. "I'm not you. Or Amber," I muttered.

"Well, there's no need to get lippy, Olivia," Mum said in her hurt voice. "Love, come on. Sometimes you've got to know your limits. It's unrealistic. I think you know as well as I do that someone like you isn't cut out to be a vet."

'Courage,' I told myself, thinking of the red thread around my wrist.

"My science teacher thinks I can do it," I told Dad in a low voice.

He put the paper down. "Science is one thing, Liv. Studying out of books. You've always been a bookworm, I'll give you that. But the reality? Putting down pets? Sewing up moggies all day? Do you really want to spend the rest of your life with your hand up a cow's backside?"

"Peter." Mum tutted.

I held firm.

Dad raised a tired eyebrow. "Alright, tell me about this work experience," he said impatiently.

"We're meant to do work experience after Christmas. I want to do it on a farm. Just let me do it. I'll prove to you I've got what it takes. If I'm no good on the farm, or if I don't get the grades at school, then forget it, but let me at least try."

"Olivia?" came Mum's exasperated voice. "I've already spoken to Sheila Staves about getting you into her office for your work experience, to do the photocopying, answer the phones and what have you."

I resisted the urge to say something sarcastic. After all, that was her idea of heaven.

"Peter?" Mum demanded.

Miraculously Dad didn't reply but turned to me instead. "Are you sure this is what you want, Olivia?"

I nodded.

"Well," said Mum, sounding put out, "seems like I'm wasting my breath. Over to you then, Olivia. We'll talk about this vet thing again when you've got your exam results. I just hope you don't end up disappointed."

"Thank you!" I yelled, and, with the biggest grin, I ran out the door to catch the school bus before they could change their minds.

17 – When the Moor Wind Blows From the West

It rained every day for the next few weeks but even the wet weather couldn't dampen my spirits. I did a bit of asking around, to see if I could find some work experience on a farm, but no one seemed to want a fifteen-year-old girl. I wasn't too worried. There was loads of time to sort it out. And, of course, I was still spending my weekends at Annie's so I was getting a lot of experience with her animals. She'd not managed to patch up her roof so I spent a lot of time emptying the full bowls of rainwater that collected under the dripping ceiling. Fortunately, the rain seemed to be keeping the bullies away and there had been no more visits.

I still went walking in the hills. I liked to watch the dark clouds roll across the sky and feel the hard spatter of raindrops blow across my cold cheeks, stinging them numb and pink. Sometimes when I was walking, I would round a corner and see Robert Enticott striding towards me, with dark eyes flashing. Of course, it wasn't real, it was all in my mind, but it was a good fantasy. Actually, I was worried about accidentally bumping into Robert as he went about his farm chores. His surliness scared me and I hated him for the things he'd said about Annie. If he ever did run into me, he'd probably say something sarcastic and I'd scuttle off and hide. So it was fortunate, really, that our paths never crossed.

Finally, one day in late October, the sun came out, and a warm west wind blew in. October should have been raw and bleak, but this was a spring-like wind, the kind that came with primroses. It was all wrong for this time of year, but at least it meant I could get out into the hills.

The warm wind slid over Rowan Hill as I climbed to the top. A low sun lit up the autumn oaks in the valley like a stage set, and the lichen on their bark glowed an unreal green. I had come to wait for another sign.

I hadn't heard the voice here or seen a single chick since the one Nell had given me, but I hadn't forgotten them, far from it. I lay on the grass within the ruined walls and tried to logic it out. The rowans' leaves flickered as I pondered out loud. It was easy to imagine them listening.

"The chicks on the doorstep were obviously left by these people who are pestering Annie. But how about the ones on the hill? How did they get here? Perhaps they've escaped from somewhere and come up here to die. Or perhaps an animal, a fox maybe, is bringing them. But from where? Then there is the voice." I glanced around me. It seemed rude to be doubting it, up here where I'd first heard it. I didn't want to provoke it, or scare it away.

"Perhaps there's some weird weather condition that makes the wind sound like a voice … I suppose I could have a brain tumour that's making me hear things but that's a bit unlikely at my age. So perhaps I'm mad. But I don't feel mad, and, anyway, Annie said she'd heard it too, so that would make her mad as well, and though she's a bit batty with all her charms and stuff, in other ways she seems quite sane."

Pretty soon I had run out of possibilities. I lay on the earth, looking up at the wide expanse of sky. A strange, gripping, tingling sensation marked the dawning realisation that there was another, totally illogical explanation. That the voice from the hill was real. It was the hill itself speaking to me. My mind went blank at the idea. But I didn't feel scared. I looked up into the blue with a new sense of wonder.

What if you just accepted that life was never going to make sense? Could you live that way? I'd been so dismissive about Annie's hocus-pocus, but admitting the voice opened the door to the possibility of believing all the other things Annie had told me. Looking back, it was when Annie wrapped that thread around my wrist that something in my thinking shifted. 'It doesn't always make sense, but that doesn't stop it being powerful,' she had said. Maybe it was just confidence trickery, maybe it worked because you believed it so you acted differently. But if it worked, why deny it? By trusting Annie's charm, in a small way, I had started to suspend my disbelief, to see what happened if I acted like the magic was true. And so far, despite my fears, my world hadn't dissolved into chaos.

Lying there I found that if I really tuned in my senses, I could feel fragments of that pulsing power I'd experienced on the hill. Of course, it could be that the energy was really coming from me, from my wanting to feel it, but if I closed my eyes, it was easy to imagine the stones beneath me, glowing in the earth. What if it wasn't my imagination? What if it was true? When at last I stood, I felt alert and energised, as if some kind of charge had flowed into me.

On the way back I got lost. I found a high hedge running all the way along the bottom of the field and couldn't get through. I was forced to follow its length until I got to a gate. Then the same again; the hedges were too high to see over, and I got disorientated, sent off at right angles. The hedges were funnelling me further and further away from my destination, but I wasn't concerned. I decided to trust my intuition. It was telling me to follow where they led and I got the feeling they were leading me somewhere important, perhaps to the answers to my questions.

Just as the dusk was beginning to gather, I found myself skirting a copse of beech, holly and birch trees. The wood beckoned. I hesitated, feeling drawn towards the cover of the trees, but wondering what hid within. A patch of vivid red stood out against the beech mast: a fly agaric toadstool. I climbed the fence – they were rare and Annie would be pleased to top up her supply. The red cap was fresh and shiny, covered in raised white patches that looked like sugar frosting on a cake. I knew better than to eat it though. If it didn't kill you, it would send you crazy with mind-bending hallucinations. Annie used it, as village people had for years, as a fly killer; a piece floating in milk would kill flies better than any aerosol. Suddenly a blackbird gave a warning call.

Fox holes covered the hillside here in a warren of tunnels. The rank tang of fox was suddenly overwhelming. And, over the fox-smell, something more. All at once I found I could pick out each different smell as if I were the fox myself: the sharp odour of grass, the alcoholic reek of rotting fruit, the dank smell of leaf mould.

It was then I saw her, the fox. Or perhaps she let me see her. She must have been watching me and waiting. She was lean and reddish brown; her sharp, pointed noise twitched. She was carrying something in her mouth. She bent her head to place it on the leaves before her, then turned to me, unafraid. With a jolt, I realised what she had been carrying. It was a chick. She fixed me with bright brown eyes.

'*Olivia.*'

That voice again, deep, insistent, inhuman. And this time it was the fox that had spoken. A fit of shivering came over me and my legs crumpled. She started at my sudden movement, her animal-self again. Quickly she picked up her meal and slunk down into the dark. When I'd stopped shaking enough to be able to stand, I ran all the way home.

Overnight the weather turned wet and dank. On the school bus the next morning, the younger kids were drawing faces in the condensation on the windows. Robert grunted to Wadsy across the aisle. Something about their conversation made my ears prick up.

"Scrawny-looking thing, Jack said. Reckon it was her that got in the hen sheds last week. Ten chickens she killed, didn't even take none," Robert said.

"Ha. Not so cheerful down at Cheerful Chickens now, then."

"No. The big boss had a right barney at him. Jack reckons Lower Gillett's lost nearly fifty birds this year."

Lower Gillett, the farm Jack managed, was a chicken farm? Why had I never known that?

Wadsy shrugged. "What does he care? He's got bloody thousands of birds in there, you'd think he could spare a few."

One of my questions had been answered. I knew where the chicks were coming from. Now what was I meant to do?

18 – Departed Spirits Have No Rest

By the time I got back from school that day it was nearly dark. I had my key in the lock of my front door, and I was looking forward to collapsing in front of some bad TV with a cup of tea, when something made me hesitate, something in the pit of my stomach, something bleak and fearful that tugged me towards Annie's. A few months ago, I would have ignored such an illogical premonition. Not now. *'She's sick, hurt – dead,'* it warned me. I grabbed a torch from the hallway. As I set off at a jog through the sodden dark, the spittering raindrops were drawn to its beam like flies. The fields were saturated with water and the run-off was setting small streams trickling down the roads. A barn owl screeched a rasping cry that made my hair stand on end.

At the end of the lane, I expected to see the welcoming lights of Annie's cottage, but everything was dark. I let myself in the back door and called Annie's name. I was surprised to find the house cold. In the dark something rushed towards me.

"Pip!" I gasped.

He was frantically pleased to see me, but when I picked him up, he was cold and shivering. I had a horrible wave of dread. I would open the kitchen door and find Annie's body.

"Annie!" I called, and overcame my fear to push open the door. The smell of wax thickened the air but no candles glowed. I stumbled against something and saw that the bowls were back on her kitchen floor, catching the drips from her leaky roof. The smell of damp permeated everything.

In the centre of the table, the silver bowl, brim-full of black water, glimmered in my torch beam. It was decorated with silver leaves and jet berries; when I looked closer, I saw the leaves formed weird faces with piercing eyes. I had to drag my eyes from it, but when I did, I saw the table had been set with three places. I moved closer; in two of the places were picture frames. One was a photograph of Annie's mother, the other her husband.

I was getting scared now. Annie was nowhere to be found. Just then I heard a muffled banging. I rushed outside and there, in the dark, up a ladder with a torch, I found her, trying to nail a piece of tarpaulin to the roof. She scowled at me as I held the ladder for her to climb down. Her face was covered with black streaks.

"As if it weren't enough having gert great holes in me roof, the electric's off and now the fire's gone out and I can't get it lit again." She took me through to her cold living room where Nell, Pip and Noggin milled around me anxiously. "Everything's damp. Even the matches. I don't know if I can get through another winter like this."

A great spasm of coughing overtook her, and when it was finished, she put her face into her hands, and her shoulders shook with silent sobbing.

I had to do something. It was too awful to hear her so desperate.

"Wait, Annie, don't worry. We'll get a fire lit, I'll go out the back and get kindling," I told her. I wrapped her in my coat and ran out to the shed to fetch newspaper and small sticks. "The shed's dryer than the house, this'll catch in no time," I told her in my brightest voice. But the matches were useless. The heads crumbled off as I struck them and by that point Annie had got so dejected that I was getting desperate too. I took a twig between my palms and started spinning it into a piece of powdery dry pine, the way I'd seen on the internet. Nell looked worried; she was trying to lick some spirit back into the old woman.

"I'm not going into no home, nor no sheltered accommodation, whatever they call it," Annie was muttering bleakly. "They tell you they're looking after you but it's like a living death in those places. Everyone sitting in a circle, too deaf or too crazy to talk to each other, heating on so hot you can't breathe, television on so loud you can't think. They call 'em senile, but when no one's listening you got to keep talking so as you don't forget who you are. I seen 'em looking out the windows of them homes on the sea front at Seaton – lost, they was. I ain't going into no home."

By now my hands were red and sore. I focused all my energy twirling the stick, willing it to make heat to warm Annie. I sprinkled bits of tissue paper into the glowing pit and they started to catch. Was it my effort or my will or a mixture of both? Quickly I added some dry kindling and to my amazement the fire bloomed alight. Annie stopped talking and sat wide eyed. Now I was like a demented person, adding twigs and splinters to my newborn fire. Soon I was able to add larger pieces of wood and the heat of the fire spread throughout the room. The dogs huddled close.

Annie looked at her lap. "Silly old fool I am, getting in such a state 'cos me fire's gone out. You done a good job there, girl."

I left Annie warming while I got the range going and made hot sweet tea.

"This time of year, there's a crack between the seasons," she told me, sipping her tea. "I got cold and scared and I reckon some of my spirit got sucked in. Not like me to get afraid like that. Your fire seems to have brought me back though. Time was, I was looking after you," Annie noted shrewdly. "You're growing up, girl. Will you join me for a meal?"

Now the room was warm and the candles lit, the sight of the old photographs sitting waiting to be served didn't seem so eerie. Annie dished up stew.

"Why are the photos at the table?" I asked.

"At Samhain, what you call Halloween, they say the veil is thin between this world and the next, so I sit with the ones who've gone on before me and I remember them over a meal. I ain't no more afraid of them dead than I was alive. In my book, there ain't no such thing as heaven or hell."

I looked at the photograph of Annie's mother. She had a sweet face and soft curly hair. There was something in her expression I couldn't read though. "What was she like?" I asked.

"She was strong," replied Annie, looking for the word. "She could look at you and straightaway know what the problem was and how to help. Not one to stay at home or hide away in the kitchen. Drove my father mad. Said it weren't right that she should go out alone to help with births. She said, 'Alright, I'll take Annie along too, then.' I was no older than you when I helped at my first birthing."

She sensed my next question, picking up Ted's photo and stroking it tenderly. In the candlelight I saw her as a young woman; she had a strong nose, high cheekbones, and the flame of the candle returned the colour to her white curls.

"Couldn't have a baby myself. Funny that, isn't it? All those herbs, and not one of 'em could make a child for me and Ted. It was hard on him. He was a farmer, through and through, and what farmer doesn't see himself with a strong boy to take over the farm? But he never chided me for it. 'Just as likely it's summat wrong with me as you,' he'd say. And then I got too old for it anyway and, well, not long beyond that, poor Ted passed on. I was sorry not to have given him the joy of a child. He was a good man."

She had grown quiet and thoughtful. It was time to leave her alone with her memories. Whether or not the dead really returned, I didn't know, but I was glad Annie got some comfort thinking about them.

Dad was sitting at the kitchen table when I got in, looking pale and grim. I poured myself a glass of milk and sat with him. He'd had his hair cut short so you could see the whorls of growth at his scalp. Soon he would be completely grey. He'd grown the grizzly stubble into a neat beard. I hated it. It was another thing for him to hide behind. Though I suppose, with my long hair, I was a fine one to talk.

"Where's Mum?" I asked.

He tried to joke but his voice was flat and expressionless. "Parish council meeting. Or was it the tennis club fundraiser? I lose track. Since I'm such a misery, she's decided to keep herself busy. She misses that job of hers, I suppose."

"Sorry I'm late. I was studying at Sadie's," I lied. "Her mum gave me a lift back."

"You're a hard worker, Olivia. It's not everyone who has a vocation. You remind me of myself in some ways. Ever since I was a little boy, I dreamt about becoming a police officer. Never a doubt in my mind that that was what I'd end up doing. Best job in the world. But working hard, doing the right thing, it doesn't always get rewarded. I just wouldn't want you to be disappointed. You see, life doesn't always turn out the way you think, does it?" His face got ugly. "Those people, those thieves. One of them got a year, the other a suspended sentence. What did I get? Years of this. There's no justice, when it comes down to it. It's a hard life, Olivia."

A little fleck of white spit had formed in the corner of his mouth, caught in the hairs of his beard. He saw me staring at it and wiped it hurriedly away. It made me feel wretched to see him like this. He was making a prison for himself, inside the house and inside his head and I could feel him sucking me into his dark, desperate world.

I wanted to shout at him, 'Come up to my hilltop, Dad. Feel the energy of the earth, and the air. Shake yourself out of this. Even now, at the dark time of the year, can't you see how wonderful the world is?'

But he wouldn't see, and I didn't know how to get through to him. I knew that if I did say anything it'd only meet with his scorn.

Winter

19 – When the Wheel Has Turned to Yule

I was spending pretty much every minute of free time I had at Annie's farm. I was getting more confident with the animals, and Annie said I was getting the hang of the herbs. I threw myself into learning in the hope that soon something would click and I'd finally be ready to understand the mysteries of the hill. I didn't know what else to do.

"Patience," soothed my teacher. "It'll come."

I found out where Lower Gillett Farm was, the home of Cheerful Chickens. It was only about a mile away. I cycled past it, doing some detective work. I didn't dare get too close in case anyone saw me snooping, but I stopped my bike in the lane and had a good look. There was no sign of the owner, Oliver Jenkins, but the place was busy with workers in blue overalls going in and out of the big wooden sheds, washing things with power hoses, loading white trucks with eggs. That meant it could be any one of a hundred people putting the chicks on Annie's doorstep. Loads of local people were employed there, apparently.

Fortunately, Annie's nasty visitors were still keeping their distance. I allowed myself the hope that they'd finally given up. They couldn't go on forever, could they? How the chicks got to the hill was still a riddle to me.

Then, one day, the week before Christmas, I was leaning my bike against the wall of Annie's cottage when I noticed a big cardboard box on her doorstep. It was wrapped in gold Christmas paper with a bow on top. The handwritten label was addressed to her and there were no stamps on it. That meant it must have been delivered by hand. I froze, staring at it. The only visitors to the cottage, apart from me and Jack, were Annie's unwelcome ones. So, they were back. What had they done now? What nasty thing had they put inside the box? I pulled a bamboo stick from a flower bed and poked it. I was relieved to find it felt almost empty. I checked to see that Annie was nowhere near, then crouched and ripped open the wrapping.

Inside the box was a mask and a hat: cheap, flimsy things, the kind of stuff you'd buy at Halloween. The rubber mask was green. It had a long nose with a wart on it. The hat was tall and black and pointed. I shut the lid on them, crushed the box with my foot, and took it straight to the bonfire at the bottom of the garden to be burnt.

Annie was cheerful. She'd made cups of strong tea that steamed in the cold air. As we got on with tending to the animals, I heard her across the yard, whistling Christmas carols. I bit my lip. I didn't want to spoil things by telling her about the gift. When all the chores were done, we went walking through the oak wood, looking for greenery to decorate her cottage with.

"You all ready for the big day then?" she asked.

"Suppose so. Mum's still fussing about the Christmas crackers matching the napkins. Amber's arriving soon. You'd think the queen was visiting from the way Mum's been getting ready. I wish I could spend the day with you instead. Are you sure you won't be lonely?" I'd been worrying about her being on her own.

"Oh, I'm alright. I got my own way of celebrating," said Annie. "Oh, there's a bit with lots of berries."

Annie paused with her hands round a branch; she seemed to be whispering something to the tree. Then she sawed the branch off cleanly. She touched the white wood before handing the branch to me. We sang 'The Holly and the Ivy' as we carried our swag of evergreens into Annie's house, my voice thin and reedy and hers deep and husky.

"The rising of the sun,
And the running of the deer ..."

It was a relief to come in out of the cold.

"Got to have lots of greenery. Helps keep the spirit of growing things alive. Helps keep the wheel of the seasons moving lest the cold freeze it still. You got a Christmas tree?"

"A fake one. Mum says a real one would shed needles on her new carpets."

Annie snorted. "That isn't the same thing at all. Put the ivy on the mantle over there and let's get a Yule log burning."

I helped her stoke up the fire.

"You hungry? I've been cooking."

She had made a cake full of nuts and dried fruit. The ornate silver bowl I'd seen on the table at Samhain was full of sweet cider, mixed with grated apple and spices.

"Wassail." She gestured, suddenly struggling for breath. She managed to pass the bowl to me before one of her terrible coughing fits overcame her.

Amber arrived on Christmas Eve in a cloud of perfume, loaded with bags of presents.

"It's nice to be earning; gives me an excuse to do more shopping." She giggled. "Are you going to come up to town for the sales, Mum? We could make a proper trip of it, maybe go and get a manicure while we're at it?"

Amber's nails were French manicured: beige to match the upholstery with a tiny sliver of white at the tip. She ran them through her new blonde highlights.

Mum hugged her, squealing, "It's so good to *seeeee* you!"

Amber had landed on her feet, she said. She was nanny to a four-month-old little girl, Maia, who was the *sweeeetest* baby you could imagine. Maia's parents were lawyers and they lived in this *huuuuge* house in West London, where Amber had her own apartment. Maia's dad was really into art and there were, like, all these *amaaazing* paintings on the walls. Next summer the family were going to take her with them on holiday to Tuscany for a month. Maia's mum was *suuuper* nice and had made Amber really welcome. It was the *best* job *ever*.

"There's a futon if you want to stay, Liv," Amber offered. Maybe absence did make the heart grow fonder.

At supper, Dad and I were mainly spectators to Mum and Amber's giggling. Dad was quiet and pale. I didn't think Amber had noticed, but some time after midnight, just after I had fallen asleep, she crept in and turned the light on. I frowned into the brightness.

"If you carry on making faces like that, you'll need Botox by the time you're twenty. And those eyebrows. You look like a cave woman," she told me, perching on the end of my bed. "You should get them plucked. I'll do it for you if you like."

"No thanks," I replied. As if I would let her near me with a pair of tweezers.

"Is he still doing it, then?" she asked.

"Yes. Every night," I confirmed. "Haven't you noticed the bags under our eyes?"

"But why?"

"It's called PTSD. When he fell in the canal, he was so scared the adrenaline made a sort of pathway in his brain that means he keeps reliving the accident. That's why he can't talk about it without getting stressed, why he can't sleep and why he goes on about everything being so dangerous all the time. It's called hyper-vigilance."

"Alright, brain-box, I don't need all the details. I meant, why isn't he better yet? I thought Devon was meant to cure him."

"Dunno." I shrugged.

"I'll make sure I put my earplugs in then." She went back to her room.

'Happy Christmas to you, too,' I thought.

Next day, we unwrapped our presents. I'd played it safe and bought smellies for everyone. Amber had bought us all smellies too, only hers were branded. I nearly gagged when she encouraged us all to have a squirt. I'd only had one thing on my Christmas list: a pair of wellies. My old boots leaked and what I really wanted were a pair of dark green wellies, ones I could wear to Annie's, and maybe to work experience. But given her feelings about the countryside, they were the last thing Mum would want me to see me in, and it was her who always did the Christmas shopping.

'If Amber hadn't made me open the disgusting perfume I could have sold it online and bought myself some boots,' I thought glumly.

But then Mum reached behind the tree for one final gift. "Look what's hiding over here. Ooh, it's got your name on Olivia. This is from us."

I blushed and felt bad. The package was heavy and I felt the flexible legs of a pair of Wellingtons inside. I was really excited as I ripped the paper off. But when I saw the boots, my face fell. They were bright pink, with a leopard print design. Festival boots, not farming boots. If it was the thought that counted then Mum's thoughts about me took clear shape in these hideous boots. They were a present for the daughter she wished she had.

"Well, I tried, Olivia." Mum sighed when she saw my face. "Honestly, I don't know why I bothered! Take them back if you don't like them. I kept the receipt." She looked all flushed and I thought she might cry.

Dad raised a warning eyebrow at me.

"No, they're great. Thanks, Mum," I managed to mutter. I would never *ever* wear them.

We sat down to lunch.

"But what do you *do* here, Mum? I mean, for fun?" asked Amber.

"Well, there's the pub, I suppose. I've been a few times for drinks with the tennis club. There are big cinemas in Exeter and Taunton."

"But they're both twenty miles away. What about eating out, spa days, window shopping? You used to love all those things."

Mum gave Amber a look as Dad came in with the turkey. Amber turned her attention to me. "So what about you, Liv? Do you go into Exeter with your mates then?"

"Not really." I squirmed. "I just, kind of, hang around here."

Mum had the bird speared with the carving fork while Dad carved slices off it, piling our plates high with thick slabs of meat. Amber was helping herself to roast potatoes, choosing all the crispiest ones.

"But doing what? I mean, what exactly is there to do round here?" she asked looking genuinely confused.

"Walking. In the hills. I like it here," I mumbled. I sounded like a right loser.

"She's got a friend in Otteridge she spends most of her free time with, cycles her bike over to see her, don't you? When are we going to meet this Sadie?" Mum asked.

At least she doesn't know about my visits to Annie's, I thought. She'd probably think Annie was loopy, that she was brain-washing me. And if she saw the state of the house she'd completely freak out.

"Olivia doesn't show much interest in going out of an evening," Dad noted. "Not like you at her age."

"You were a party animal from the word go," Mum teased Amber wistfully. "I could never keep track of the invites you used to get."

"Nothing's changed there." Amber giggled. "But seriously, Liv, don't you want to go out in the evenings with your school friends? Meet boys? What do the locals do?"

"Well, actually there's a Young Farmers' do in the village at New Year. Mum, I meant to ask ..."

"Oh, brilliant!" Amber hooted. "I bet they all have a good knees-up, drinking cider and dancing to The Wurzels. Honestly, Liv, you don't know what you're missing in London." She clasped Mum's arm. "I went to this club in the West End a few weeks ago. You'd have loved it, Mum. It was so classy. We had cocktails, then there was a floor show with dancers, and they had these enormous fish tanks in the wall with real mermaids. I mean not real, obviously, but trained swimmers dressed up like mermaids and there were all sorts of celebrities there too. We nearly managed to get into the VIP zone because Pippa knew one of the bouncers ..." And she regaled us for the next ten minutes with Amber's adventures in the big city.

Mum egged her on, sighing and cooing. I don't think they noticed how quiet Dad had grown. I cleared our greasy plates. As I brought through the trifle, I heard that Dad had changed the topic.

"You see it worst in the city, this broken society we live in. Or you would, Amber, if you weren't so blinded by the bling and bright lights. The beggars, the nutters, the gangs, all just wandering the streets looking for trouble. You're earning, you've got a bit of cash to spend, you're having fun and that's only right. But there's a lot of young people out there who seem to think that the world owes them the latest phone and a pair of trainers, that working's beneath them. Crime's changed – when I first joined the force the criminals were drug addicts, or desperate in some way; crime was easier to understand. Now there's this casual, 'I want it, I'll take it'. And it doesn't stop at theft. I worry about you out every night. Tell me you don't use unlicensed mini-cabs, Amber."

"No, Dad," sighed Amber spooning out trifle and rolling her eyes. This 'Youth of Today' speech was something we'd been subjected to since Dad's accident. He seemed to have aged by about a hundred years.

"I thought that coming down here we would avoid the worst of it. But just look at the local paper and you can see it's spread down here too. Young people nowadays thinking farming's beneath them and getting into petty crime instead. The get-rich-quick mentality. No effort required on their part, no obligation to give anything back. More, bigger, cheaper, me, me, me. It can only end in disaster."

Amber looked up at the ceiling.

"The things I read. Out of control, some of these local lads. No, you can't escape the fact that this society is sick. I've come to the conclusion that all you can do is keep your head down and look after your own."

We sat in silence for a bit. Yet again Dad had killed the mood. Mum looked so dejected that I felt a rush of guilty sympathy for her.

"Coffee? What's on television this afternoon?" she asked brightly, trying to change the subject.

Dad went to have a nap after lunch while we cleared up. I stacked the clean dinner service away in the dresser in the living room. Amber and Mum spoke in lowered voices as they washed and dried with their backs to me. Their blonde, highlighted heads were touching and they looked more like sisters than mother and daughter.

"If you're miserable, Mum, why don't you just move back?"

"He won't, Amber. You heard him. He thinks London is this den of vice, and the only safe place to be is stuck out here in this godforsaken wilderness."

"But if he never goes out, never talks about what happened, what does it matter where he lives? He's not going to get any better at this rate, is he? I hate to think of you being so unhappy, Mum."

"Oh, I'm alright for the time being. He'll come round. I give him a year. And then we'll have hell to pay from Olivia. She loves it here. You've heard the vet thing?"

I could imagine Amber rolling her eyes.

"Oh, buy her a bunny rabbit, she'll soon get over it," my sister said cruelly.

My mother sighed impatiently, but then she chuckled. "A bunny rabbit. Oh, Amber, you shouldn't. Poor Livvy."

I crept away to my room. They had no idea what I had found in the countryside. I had found *me*. The reason it all felt so familiar was because it was my *home*. I belonged here. I couldn't go back. I fingered the red thread I still wore around my wrist, and a feeling of bleak freedom sparked in me. I would show them. All I needed was to find a farm that would take me for work experience. What was it Sadie had said? 'You can't let things just *happen* to you, Liv. You've got to *make* them happen.'

20 – Love Will Kiss Thee On the Mouth

Mum had somehow persuaded Dad to join her at the Staves' New Year's Eve party and Amber had gone back to London, which meant that Sadie and I had the house to ourselves. Giggling, we helped ourselves to a small glass of sherry each. I was feeling warm and reckless. I turned the stereo up loud and Sadie and I grooved and bounced on my bed like kids.

"Is this dress too much? Can you see my bum?" Sadie said, wiggling her bottom in the mirror.

"Disgusting!" I shouted, chucking a pillow at her.

She shrieked and chucked it back. She looked amazing. Her tight green slip dress set off her straightened auburn hair perfectly, and unlike me she had curves.

"Look at your legs, you bitch. I'd kill for legs like that. Shame I can't get you out of black," she sighed.

"Can't I wear something over the top?" I said. My little black dress was sleeveless, short and clingy and I was feeling a bit naked.

"No, you bloody can't. Chest out, tummy in."

"What chest?" I moaned, peering at my non-existent bust.

"Oh shut up. You look like a supermodel," reassured Sadie. "You … still not started yet?" she asked casually.

"No," I replied miserably. "Mum says if I haven't started by the summer, she's going to have to take me to a specialist for an investigation."

"God. Like a gynaecologist?"

"Yep." I winced. In my imagination, the gynaecologist was a man and he was putting on latex gloves. "Do you think I should be worried?"

"I dunno. I expect it's alright," Sadie said unconvincingly. "Anyway, enjoy it while you can. Periods are such a pain. And as for boobs, if I get one more comment from Wadsy ..." She stuck her fingers down her throat and we fell in helpless laughter on the bed.

"Oh, God, Sadie. What are we letting ourselves in for?" I wondered, when we'd recovered.

"We'll soon find out. Young farmers, here we come."

The hall was decked out in lights. I wished myself invisible, and pulled my hair over my face as we shuffled though the queue, the music thumping out into the still, cold night. The place was packed; I felt clumsy and prickly with self-consciousness. I'd not socialised much in the village and the thought suddenly struck me that somewhere in the crowd might be the boys who were bullying Annie. I clung to Sadie's arm as we inched through the beery crowd. I began to look about. To my relief, no one gave us a second glance. I even recognised a few faces from the years above me at school. Most of them were older.

"I can see Wadsy at the bar," Sadie shouted. "He owes us a drink."

We squeezed round the edge of the dance floor and prised our way into the scrum of bodies near the bar. Wadsy gave a huge thumbs-up and a kind of roar when he saw us. Two drinks were passed back to us. Some sort of sweet whisky and lemonade. Wadsy must have smuggled the whisky in as they surely wouldn't have sold it to him at the bar. Whatever. We chinked glasses.

"Cheers. Happy New Year, honey!" shouted Sadie. "Ooooh. I love this song. Come and dance!"

At first, I felt like my arms and legs were made of stiff cardboard and that the whole room was watching me. I kept tugging the hem of my dress down, but the whisky and Sadie's enthusiasm and the music got to me and soon I started to enjoy myself. We did silly ballroom and disco moves. We danced till we were sweaty and breathless.

Sadie grabbed my arm and pointed. "Robert's here. I'm going to talk to him."

My stomach rolled as I caught sight of him. He was wearing jeans and a white T-shirt, looking even more unbelievably handsome out of his school uniform. Sadie had already set off across the floor, weaving through the drunken dancers.

"Don't leave me. I'm coming too!" It was the first time I had ever seen Robert properly smiling. It changed him. Despite our conversation on the playing field, I felt oddly pleased to see him. Knowing him gave me the right to be here. He was in the centre of everything. Everyone loved him. His back was slapped, an arm gripped his shoulder, a drink was passed on to him. Someone clapped him in a hug. He looked relaxed; he was surrounded by friends, cousins, part of a community. Things at the farm must have been pretty bad to make him think of leaving all this. He caught sight of me and Sadie and mimed astonishment at our outfits.

"I thought Wadsy had put you off Young Farmers. What d'you reckon?" He grinned.

"It's brilliant!" yelled Sadie, using the noise as an excuse to get closer to him. Under his T-shirt you could see his muscly arms; Sadie wobbled on her heels and held on to him to steady herself. She knew all the tricks.

"Not as cool as London clubs, I bet." Robert raised an eyebrow at me.

"Don't ask me. I reckon this is much more fun!" I shouted back. It was true. I was having fun. I didn't have to worry about looking cool. No one was judging me. The New Year was less than an hour away and I was excited about it. I sipped my drink.

Robert eyed it, tutting but approving. "And you a police officer's daughter," he teased.

"Come and dance," Sadie begged him, but he shrank away, looking horrified.

"I'm a bloody awful dancer," he insisted.

"Bet you're not." She beamed and boogied off a little way before joining a group of dancers who welcomed her in with whoops. I watched Robert watching her. Sexy Sadie. She would eat him alive. I had a spasm of envy. Why had I even let myself imagine he might fancy me? He was much too beautiful for me. I would never be in with a chance.

"I don't know how she does it!" I yelled to Robert. "I wish I had her confidence."

He chuckled. "You're alright, Liv," he shouted. Then he looked guiltily to the floor. "That day by the swings, I was being a bastard."

I was surprised to hear him say it, but I couldn't help but answer, "Yes, you were."

"Yeah, well, sorry."

Either the whisky, or his apology made my cheeks burn. We stood together watching the heaving dance floor. Just then, across the room, I noticed a couple of older men gesticulating to Robert. One was tall, with a swelling beer belly, the other shorter, skinny, but both were swarthy with dark brows and strong, jutting noses. Brothers, or cousins at the very least. They seemed to be pointing in my direction. I didn't like the way they looked at me. I edged closer to Robert. He waved them away angrily and they went back to the bar, shooting surly glances over their shoulders.

"What was that about?" I shouted.

"Nothing." He shook his head. "Don't matter."

"No, tell me," I shouted over the music. My mouth was almost next to his ear now.

"You said you didn't want to hear no more about Annie Tilke."

"This is about Annie? God. Even here?"

"Ain't as simple as that, Liv. Who you spend your time with, that's your business, but those blokes over there, they're Tremaynes. They reckon it's their business too."

"What are you on about? Who the hell are the Tremaynes? Are they the ones behind this?" I asked him.

Robert looked at me blankly. "Behind what?" he asked, bewildered.

"Maybe it's about time you realised exactly how much abuse she's been putting up with. It's intimidation!"

"I don't know what you're talking about and I don't know nothing about no intimidation. All I mean is that if you're a friend of Annie Tilke, you're no friend of theirs."

"But why?"

"You mean you still don't know what she did?" he asked, looking horrified.

"What do you mean?" I retorted angrily, but the expression on his face gave me a cold feeling in my belly. "All this stupid witch stuff?"

"No, no. There's something else. Something worse, much worse than that."

I stood rooted to the spot, stunned by this new information.

"Look, I thought you knew. I thought you must have heard the gossip by now. Perhaps it's best you ask her. I don't want to be the one to tell you."

People around us were beginning to pay attention to our argument and it made me flustered. "Perhaps I will." I hissed and pushed my way out of the hall. I felt hot and irritable and suddenly unwelcome.

"Olivia!" Robert called after me.

The cold sobered me up quickly. I walked across the grass, skirting the hall. I was making for the cricket pitch, a big, wide, open space where I could get my head straight and process all this new information. It would have been easy to reject what Robert had said outright, were it not for the small unwelcome memory of something Annie had said: 'Maybe you want to go and ask them gossips in the village why? Then perhaps you won't want to come no more neither.' I hadn't gone far, though, when I noticed the ember of a cigarette burning in the dark.

"Liv!" called Wadsy. At least he was pleased to see me. "Young Farmers is bloody brilliant, isn't it. You having a good time? You look amazing. I'm having a bloody mental time with me mates. Why ain't you dancing with Sadie? Ah. You giving her a chance to make her moves on Robsy? Good girl. He's a lucky boy. Sit down here with me. I'm knackered. Reckon I been dancing and drinking flat out since we got here. Here, I got some whisky, you want some?"

"No, thanks."

"Reckon I'm gonna have a bloody terrible hangover in the morning. Worth it though. You having a good time? I'm having a bloody mental time!" he repeated.

'Drunk people are so boring,' I thought. I listened to him gabble for a bit. I was getting cold. Just as I was about to get up to go, the DJ put on a slow tune. It was an old one. It made me feel a bit sad. It would be nice to be held to that tune. I thought of Sadie snuggling up to Robert and I tried to be pleased for her. Wadsy looked pensive too. Before I could move away, he laid his head on my shoulder.

After a bit he looked up at me with eyes that could barely focus. "Don't suppose you'd give us a kiss?' he asked. Even in his drunkenness he could read the look that crossed my face. "No, sorry, course not. You're a nice girl, Liv. Too good for me, I know that."

"Sorry, Wadsy, I just don't ..."

"No, I ain't fishing for compliments, I know what I am. A bloody mess. I ain't never had no luck with females. I should ask Robert what the trick is. That Sadie, she's gorgeous. He'd be crazy to pass that up."

"Yeah, they'll make a good couple," I agreed flatly.

Wadsy heaved his head off my shoulder and peered at me. "Oh, bloody hell. Don't tell me he's got you too?" he drawled in disbelief. "Robert Enticott, you are a lucky, lucky man." His head fell back to my shoulder, but this time I was a pillow, not a conquest.

"No … it's not like that," I rushed to correct him. "It's obviously Sadie who should go out with him; she's gorgeous and clever and funny, whereas I'm, well …"

Wadsy was silent. I moved my shoulder to rouse him and discovered he was out cold. Inside, the countdown to midnight began, a raucous chorus. Sadie and Robert would be pressed tight in the crowd.

"Yes," I whispered as the church bells struck midnight. "Yes. He's got me too."

I started as a figure loomed out of the darkness.

"Liv! What are you doing here?" Sadie's voice was relieved. "We've been looking everywhere for you. Happy New Year. Oh!" she exclaimed with surprise. "Wadsy's here too?"

As I tried to shift Wadsy's drunken weight off my shoulder I saw that Robert was standing behind her. And the moment he saw I was with Wadsy he gave a short bark of a laugh, turned on his heel and marched back inside.

)○(

"Olivia! Sadie! It's nearly noon," called my mother from downstairs. Sadie groaned and put a pillow over her head. Then she remembered. "You were telling me the truth last night, weren't you? Absolutely nothing happened? You can tell Auntie Sadie."

"Urgh. With Wadsy? Are you joking? As if."

"Poor old Wadsy."

"Anyway, how about you? Are you really sure you didn't kiss Robert? Not even a teeny weeny one?"

Sadie sighed her disappointment and I tried to keep the relief from my face. Even if he didn't kiss Sadie, it didn't mean there was any chance for me. I was just glad I hadn't got my nose rubbed in it. I wasn't sure I could listen to her telling me what a great snog he was.

"No. I told you. Not that I didn't make it bloody obvious I was interested. He kept saying he was worried about you. It was him that suggested we look for you. I thought he might just be trying to get me outside, but no such luck. Aw, it's alright. I went off him a bit when he said he didn't dance."

I remembered the sour expressions on the Tremayne men's faces. What on earth could Annie have done for them to hate her so much? Were they the reason Robert was searching for me? If they were the ones pestering Annie, and they knew I was her friend, then perhaps I had good reason to be scared. I was still too tired to think properly. There was probably nothing in it. Perhaps Robert was just feeling guilty after our row.

"Knock, knock," said Mum at the door. "Come on, girls, up you get. Glad to see you dragged Olivia out with you last night, Sadie. You have a good time?"

"Yes." we chorused.

"Well, Olivia, I did a bit of networking on your behalf at the party last night. That work experience place you've been looking for, I've found you one. It's all set up. Sheila Staves knows a local farmer who needs some help. You can start working Saturdays, then all through the summer holidays if it suits you. Anyway, Sheila very kindly rang him this morning and it's all arranged. I think his son's at your school. Robert something?"

"Oh no," I groaned.

"Enticott, I think the name is. Oh. What have I done now? Well, really, Olivia. Sometimes I don't know why I bother!"

She shut the door on us and I heard her stomping downstairs. Sadie was grinning like a Cheshire cat. I threw a pillow at her and she shrieked.

"I'll show him," I declared. But I didn't relish the thought.

21 – Cast a Stone, the Truth to Know

"When exams are over, I've got so many plans," Sadie said. She was doing a yoga pose on my bed and had one foot almost behind her ear. For a second, she reminded me of a ginger cat cleaning itself. She broke the pose and bounced up onto her knees. She was much more of a dog than a cat, really. No good at all at hiding her feelings.

"How about camping? We could go down to the River Dart. I know this brilliant place where the water's just deep enough that you can get on a blow-up camp bed and float for ages down the river. And then we could toast marshmallows by the fire. Vegan ones, because the normal ones have cows' hooves and bones and stuff in. And I really want to make wine. Dad's got this book. I think we should make loads of elderflower wine and have a party on the beach. We could invite everyone in our year."

Sadie's enthusiasm was infectious. Although it was only the first of January, by the time Mum called us down for lunch we had already planned this year's summer of freedom.

It felt a bit dangerous introducing her to Mum and Dad. She knew so much about me and they knew so very little. But she charmed them with her outspoken opinions and her confidence. It didn't much matter whether they agreed with her, they liked her style.

After lunch, we walked the back way up to Rowan House. Even though it was New Year's day, it was still and warm in protected places. A few primroses gleamed palely in the hedgerows, peering out amongst shiny stonecrop and hart's tongue ferns. They shouldn't have shown their faces until springtime, but springtime was coming earlier and earlier according to Annie. Ahead of us a cock pheasant, a survivor of the Boxing Day shoot, darted out, running low like a man caught short for the toilet. He took flight with a metallic *charcharchar* from his beating wings.

I wanted Sadie to see my special place. I wanted her opinion on the dead chicks; I kept the secret of the voice to myself. I wouldn't know where to begin on that one, or even how to explain it to myself.

"What an amazing view!" whooped Sadie when we got to the top.

At the summit, a chill wind plastered our hair across our faces and made us shout to hear each other. It whipped away the memories of the previous evening and the conversation over lunch. It cleared my head. "Let me show you the house!" I yelled.

Inside the rowan circle it was quieter.

"Imagine living up here," Sadie enthused. "I bet you can get a really good view of the sea from the top of that pine." She tried unsuccessfully to climb it, skinning her knees and swearing while I beat through the undergrowth looking for any sign of chicks. I couldn't find any.

"Perhaps they're pheasant chicks or something," she suggested.

"No. They're yellow fluffy chicks like on Easter cards. I just don't get it. I can see why someone might put them on Annie's doorstep, to try to scare her, but I don't get why they're up here. And what's killing so many chicks in the first place."

"Hmm. You eat eggs, don't you?" Sadie said.

"Yes."

"Well, cockerels don't lay eggs. So what do you think happens to the male chicks on egg farms?"

"I've never thought about it," I realised. "Don't they get fattened up for eating?"

"No, no, no. Broiler chickens are a completely different breed. I thought you knew everything, clever-clogs."

"Hardly. God, Sadie, I didn't know that. So, what *do* they do with male chicks?"

"What do you think they do with them?" she asked impatiently. She put a hand round her neck and mimed yanking it. "No one needs male chicks."

"Oh. Right." I gulped. "Sadie, there's this egg farm near here, Cheerful Chickens. It's big. I've cycled past it a few times."

"Then that's where they're coming from."

"Yes. But it's more than a mile away. How are the chicks getting up here?"

She thought about it for a few seconds. "Dunno." She shrugged, as mystified as me.

A twist of cold wind snaked through the trees; Sadie huddled deeper inside her coat but I breathed deep its chill scent of leaf and root and stone. Suddenly I knew what I wanted to do. "Let's visit the farm," I said.

"What?"

"In secret, I mean. I want to find out for sure where the chicks are coming from," I told her. "And how they're getting up here."

Sadie's face was a sight – she looked flabbergasted to hear me make such a suggestion. "Visit the farm?" she said warily. It was usually me being sceptical of her hare-brained plans.

"Yes, you know, in the dark, without anyone seeing us. When everyone's gone home."

"Ah, I see, a little reconnaissance?" she mused. I nodded. There was a glint in her eye that told me she was interested. "It's not a bad idea, but, Liv, if someone saw us, you know it would be trespassing?" she added seriously. "Breaking and entering. If we got found out, we might get arrested. My mum did, a few times, in her animal rights days. Are you willing to risk that?"

I considered. "Would they let us into college if we got arrested?"

"Good point. I dunno."

"We'd better not get arrested then." I laughed nervously. "God, if Jack caught us there, he'd be furious. And Annie would be so angry. I mean, Jack's almost like a son to her. My dad would be pretty upset too."

My friend looked nervous. "Seriously, Liv, if it would make trouble with your family maybe we'd better not. After all, you need to keep them sweet if you want to stay here, don't you?"

"Yeah," I admitted.

Sadie looked at me steadily with one raised eyebrow. If she felt the hush, the gathering of energy that was waiting for my decision, she showed no sign of it. I really needed answers about those chicks. The answers might point me towards

Annie's bullies. They might even help me make sense of what happened on the hill.

"It would have to be very late at night," I thought aloud.

"And we could take photos. Check the conditions of the birds and stuff. I bet it's horrible in there," Sadie added casually, but I could see by the flare of her nostrils that she was fired up by the idea.

"When?" I asked.

"Well, no point rushing things," Sadie said. "Half the fun is in the planning. A couple of months should give us time to plan the perfect break-in. And at least by March it won't be so bloody cold. Are we on?"

"We're on."

As if to seal the pact, another sharp gust of wind swept through our sheltering place and bound us with a swirling eddy of leaves.

22 – Fairly Take and Fairly Give

All too soon the first day of my work experience came around. I was excited but terrified. I just couldn't afford to muck it up. On top of that, Robert would be there and I hadn't seen him since the New Year's party or dared bring up with Annie what he'd said about her. It was freezing cold and still dark. As I was unlocking my bike to leave, I stepped in a puddle and it went right through my leaky boots, soaking my socks. I groaned, and ran back indoors. Now I would be late. And the only boots I could find mocked me from the hall cupboard, pink with leopard print design.

"Get up here at 6.30," Mr Enticott had told me on the phone the previous week. "Wear summat mucky, cos you're gonna get dirty." The hum of the generator greeted me across the concrete yard. I could see lights on in the dairy.

"Hello?" I called. There was a banging, a cow kicking, I thought, and a shuffling, but no reply. I slid open the door marked 'milking parlour'; the pukey-sweet smell of milk was overpowering. A huge milk tank, fed by tubes from the dairy, was filling with a rhythmic swoosh of milk. The inner door slid open and Mr Enticott came out. He was a tall, red-faced man with curly brown hair. I wondered meanly who his son got his looks from, because it certainly wasn't his father.

"Livia, are you?" I could see him raise an eyebrow at my ridiculous boots. "Get yourself a boiler suit."

They were all way too big, but I rolled up the legs and the sleeves and tried not to think what I looked like. I'd had to tie my hair back and I felt about as ugly as it was possible to feel.

"I'll show you round the dairy. Robert's feeding the calves, he'll be back shortly."

The dairy was warm with the fug of cow-breath and steaming dung; black-and-white Friesian cows filed in on either side through a fenced walkway. Some lurched in, clattering across the concrete, while others were more sedate, their huge udders bulging with milk.

"The cows live inside this time of year. Later we'll have to clean out the stalls and bed 'em up with fresh straw," Mr Enticott told me.

In the centre of the two aisles of cows a lower trough put the person milking on a level with their rear ends as the cows ate from their stands.

"Now, watch carefully, you'll be doing this by yourself next week. First, I wash the udders with warm water, and dry 'em with a paper towel," he told me, going from cow to cow. "Next I give the teats a squeeze to check they ain't got no infections, mastitis and the like." He gently butted the cow's udder with his fist. "Gets the milk flowing. You gotta be quick with the clusters now." He reached up to pull down a set of four suction tubes attached to a cable on the ceiling. He applied them to the cow's udder and she shifted her weight, but didn't seem to mind. "Get on." He stepped back sharply as his next cow aimed a kick in his direction. "There, that weren't so bad, were it," he scolded the cow, who rolled her eyes at him grumpily. "Come down and try it out."

Down in the trough, the cows' huge bony backsides lined up to face me. I was cack-handed, and scared they would kick me. I dabbed at the udders with the wet cloth.

"Not like that, show some gumption, girl," urged Mr Enticott.

With each cow, I grew in confidence. The last cows were filing in when Robert appeared. He ignored me and went for a sack of calf feed.

"You not finished yet, boy? You're taking your bloody time, aren't you?"

If Robert heard his dad he showed no sign of having done so.

"Well, Livia, you're not bad for a first timer," Mr Enticott said as I was plugging the last cow into the clusters.

Just then, a shower of warm slurry shot from the cow's behind, splattering my shoulders and hair. I jumped back with a yelp.

"I told you you'd get mucky," laughed the farmer.

Robert stood smirking.

"Now get out back and clean up. Robert, show her where we keep the calves. And shift your arse, boy, would you?"

When I was cleaner, Robert took me to the pens behind the milking parlour without speaking. It was clear he didn't want me there. He probably thought I wasn't up to the hard work. Sod him. I needed this work experience and I was going to make a success of it, despite him. The calves stood up in their straw bedding, looking curiously at us with huge eyes and long lashes.

"How old are they?" I asked.

He looked irritated and I wondered if he was going to ignore me. "Week, two weeks," he finally muttered.

"Why aren't they with their mothers?"

He looked at me furiously. "Don't you townies know anything?" he exploded. "'Cos we need to milk their mothers so you can have your cornflakes in the morning, that's why."

"Okay. I only asked."

"Come to play at farming, have you?" he snarled. "Well, bully for you! Bit harder work than you expected, is it? Not so pretty as you thought? Don't worry, we won't be put out if you don't come back next week."

Why was he so angry with me? Tears pricked my eyes but I had nothing to lose. "Sorry to disappoint you, but I will be coming back next week, and the week afterward!" I snapped. "Why do you have to be such a grumpy git?"

That shocked him into silence. He looked a bit guilty. After a while he mumbled, "Last thing I need is you showing me up. 'Not bad for a first timer.' Do you know how hard it is to get a good word out of the old man? Can't remember when he last gave me a compliment. He hasn't been happy since the day he took over the farm from Granddad. Trying to turn it into something it ain't. Pushing and pushing. Pushing me to the bloody limit."

He ran a hand through his thick black hair and looked down at the straw. A calf tottered over and nuzzled him expectantly through the bars. I saw his hand creep into the pen and caress its silky fur, and it quivered with delight. "I heard you want to be a vet, Liv," he muttered finally.

I nodded, still embarrassed to hear something so unlikely spoken aloud. "Sadie tell you?"

"Yeah. Well, you got guts, I'll give you that. Fair play to you for coming on the farm and putting your money where your mouth is. Now help me feed these calves or we'll both have the old man after us."

We got in the pen and I held a bucket of milk while one of the younger calves plunged its nose in and slurped and snuffled. Robert took my hand and showed me how to hold my fingers under the surface of the milk to train the calf to suck properly, and I pretended it meant nothing to me that he'd touched me. "Don't you ever get attached to them?" I asked, not wanting to sound soft.

He laughed harshly. "They're not pets. It's a business. You bring 'em into the world, and you see 'em out of it. That's the arrangement."

"I see," I said quietly.

He looked down at the slurping, nuzzling calf. "Don't get me wrong. I'm a farmer, born and bred. I care for them. I try to make life easy for 'em while they're here. They're not just pieces of meat or money in the bank to me. When I start talking like that, then it's time to get out of farming."

"I thought you did want to get out of farming," I said without thinking.

In a second Robert had let go of the calf and grabbed my arm so hard I gasped. He yanked me close until his face was only inches from mine. For a stupid moment I thought he was going to kiss me. But instead he hissed, "Don't ever let me hear you talking like that in front of my father, you understand?"

I nodded and he released me, looking shocked at his own reaction. "Right then," he muttered, "I reckon Dad's got some more jobs for you."

After the cows were milked, the parlour had to be hosed down and swept clean. After breakfast the tanker would pull up in the yard to collect the milk, and when it had been driven off, the collection tank would have to be scrubbed and rinsed clean. It was already nearly nine o'clock and I was hungry. The kitchen was warm. Mrs Enticott had sausages, eggs, toast and strong tea ready for us. She was a quiet woman, dark like Robert. She only looked at me askance but I saw it was her he took after. I wondered what she made of me.

"I saw Frank Tremayne at market last week," Mr Enticott was saying to Robert. My ears pricked up at the name and I saw Robert glance over at me. "He's got the piggery up and running. Good price for pork at the moment. Sounds like he's cashing in." Mr Enticott tucked into a sausage enthusiastically. "He's bought into a corporation that guarantees him good prices. High Health pigs, he calls 'em. The whole farm's run with computers. Computers let down the feed, computers let them from one pen to the next, control the temperature. Easy life."

"Factory farming. Not my idea of what farming's about," Robert said. "That's management, not animal husbandry. Don't ever see the light of day, those pigs, 'cept maybe as they go into the truck to go for slaughter. They should be outside rooting, not sitting on concrete. Frank tell you about how they get bored and go cannibal?"

"What?"

"Yeah. I heard they pick on a weak one, kill it, then eat it. Just for something to do, shut inside all day."

"Hark at you, up on your high horse. Robert's going soft, that's his trouble," announced Mr Enticott to me, reddening.

I began to see why Mrs Enticott kept her head down; the tension between father and son crackled.

"Gotta move with the times. I'm gonna pay Frank a visit next week. You should give it some thought, Robert. This herd hasn't made no money since I don't know when. I'm thinking of the future of this farm, even if you ain't. You judging me for trying to make a profit, son?"

"That's not it. It's just ... Oh, what's the point? You never listen anyway."

Mr Enticott had successfully humiliated his son. Robert scowled, dumped his plate in the sink and slammed the door behind him. My cheeks were burning at witnessing the row, but apparently it was nothing unusual.

Mr Enticott was already cheerful again. "Don't mind him, Livia. Coming back next week, or 'as we put you off? There's always jobs to do, so when your work experience is done, why don't you give us a hand regular? My mardy son will have to lump it."

As I cycled slowly home for lunch, I began to understand why Robert was always so sullen at school. Through a gap in the hedges, I glimpsed him across the fields in his tractor. I was too far away to hear what he was shouting, but I could see him beating the steering wheel in a fury.

Spring

23 – When the Wheel Begins to Turn

We'd been planning it for months, but the time to visit Lower Gillett had finally arrived. It was a Friday night in March. I was dressed in black, my hair hidden in a dark woollen hat, crouching in a ditch with Sadie. In the warmth of Sadie's bedroom, planning our raid had felt like a game, but now my stomach was scorching with nerves. Someone had filled my innards with hot stones and I had a splitting headache. I had a bad feeling about tonight. According to Sadie, the moon was full, but a thick blanket of cloud covered it. However, there was light spilling from inside the chicken houses.

"Pass me your phone," Sadie whispered. "You ready?"

"Sadie, I don't know if I can …" I quavered. I wanted to go home and hide. I felt as flimsy as tissue paper, a liability.

"Course you can. What's the worst that can happen?"

I could think of plenty of terrible things, like getting arrested, ruining our futures, my parents deciding to move back to London since I was running so wild. And always in the back of my mind a sense of sick apprehension; would tonight answer my questions about the dead chicks? Or was I about to be led deeper into confusion? While I dithered, Sadie was already off, running low towards the perimeter of the farm. I was surprised at how pissed off with her I was. It was alright for her, with her easy-going, uncomplicated parents. God knows what Mum and Dad would say if they could see me.

I scuttled after her on weak legs. We thudded up against the slatted wooden walls of the chicken sheds, causing a few hens inside to cackle briefly. We waited. My heart was thudding in my mouth. No one came. We inched our way round the back of the building, looking for a way in. The adrenaline turned my sense of smell up to full volume: creosote and ammonia, mildewed straw, and the strange mineral smell of fresh-laid eggs.

An unlocked metal door took us inside the shed.

"No wonder he keeps losing hens to the foxes," Sadie whispered.

But I was worried. If the place was unlocked, then maybe someone was guarding it. There was no time to think though. Sadie released the bolt from the wooden inner door and we both shielded our eyes against the light.

When our vision had adjusted, I gawped at the sight before me. I had never seen so many chickens. The sheds were enormous, as big as the biggest supermarket. The birds had russet feathers, yellow legs and beaks. They were so thick on the ground that you could hardly see the sawdust bedding beneath them. They were huddled round water dispensers or heating lamps. Around the walls, hens roosted on rails and there were nesting boxes stuffed full of chickens lining the walls.

"There's nowhere near enough room for all of them," I whispered.

"Cheerful chickens, he calls them. He might as well have them in cages for all the room they have," Sadie replied, taking photo after photo.

The hens eyed us warily, but most seemed reluctant to get up.

"Poor things." Sadie knelt down and gently handled a clucking chicken. "Look at this." The chicken's legs were covered in nasty peeling blisters. "Disgusting. I've read about this. The sawdust is so full of ammonia from all the chicken poo that it makes their legs come up in blisters. That's why they aren't running away from us." Sadie took another photo. We waded through the unprotesting birds.

The chickens were so submissive. I thought of the fox that had got in. Every snap of that fox's jaws would have killed a bird; the chickens had just accepted their lot in life. The fox's teeth would have met no resistance as they slipped smoothly into flesh. For all my sympathy for them, the chickens' docility scared me. It was the thrill of being the hunter that drew me. I felt for a moment the fabulous frenzy of blood and feathers, the packed bodies spilling to either side, erupting over the fox's head as it tunnelled into the cackling crowd.

"We should go, Sadie," I urged. My feeling of unease was growing.

"What about your chicks? We haven't got what we came for yet."

We shut the door to the big barn behind us and opened another into a room full of infrared heat lamps. Thousands of chicks clustered under them, peeping quietly or scurrying between feed dispensers. But there was no sign of any dead chicks.

Sadie took some photos and we edged out of the barn. There was some farm machinery, some feed bins and a vast pit where the straw and chicken-waste went.

I heard footsteps.

"Quick, someone's coming." I hissed to Sadie and we ducked behind a digger.

A man in dark overalls let himself into the main shed. As he slipped into the door I caught a glimpse of dark hair, thinning at the temples, and a flushed, weather-beaten face – it was Jack! Sadie squeezed my arm in the dark. We were both scared now. The pains in my stomach were making me want to double up. I gripped the bucket of the digger and smelt damp earth. Then, over the smell of our own fear, I smelt the foul-sweet odour of decomposing flesh. Suddenly I knew where the dead chicks were. "Sadie. Follow me," I whispered.

We edged around the refuse pit. The earth that had been excavated to make the pit rose up behind in mounds. Sadie shielded then switched on her torch. I was terrified, knowing Jack could come back out of the shed at any minute. Sandwiched within the red soil was a layer of dead chicks, compressed by the weight of the soil that had been loaded on top of them and over the ridge, fresher, maggoty chicks scattered the surface of the earth, dug up by dogs or, more likely, foxes.

"Well, we don't know how they're getting to the hill, but we definitely know where your chicks are coming from at least." Sadie grimaced. "They gas them straight after they're hatched, probably, then bury them here. Nice." And before I could stop her, she lifted the phone, pointed and clicked. She had forgotten the flash. It lit up the whole yard. A door clattered shut inside the shed and the metal door clanged.

"Who's there?" shouted Jack and we dropped to the ground and began to crawl. As she scuttled into the open, making for the long grass, Sadie dropped my phone. I turned back, grabbed it, then rolled behind a hummock of earth for cover. From my hiding place I saw Jack pelt past me, gaining on Sadie. He made a lunge for her leg and she went sprawling into the grass. But he hadn't seen me.

"I got you! Don't you try nothin'." I heard him warn her as I cowered in my burrow. "Where's the others? You din't come here alone. What is it? Animal rights? Come on, where are your friends?"

"I don't know what you're talking about," retorted Sadie, almost managing to keep the quaver from her voice. I bit my lip so hard I tasted blood.

"Gone are they? Legged it and left you? Cowards!" Jack called out to the dark hedgerows where he assumed her accomplices were hiding, but the insult came out forced and nervous. "Trying to ruin me, are you? Well then, my little maid, you just wait till the gaffer gets here. He's gonna have my bloody guts for garters, thanks to you! Come on, up. You're gonna do some talking."

He hauled Sadie to her feet and began to frog-march her back past the shed and up to the farm.

"Oi! You don't have to hold my arm so tightly, I'm not going to run for it," I heard her shouting, the bolshie tone back in her voice. "And in case you were wondering, I've left a note, my parents know exactly where I am." Sadie could hold her own. She sounded excited rather than scared.

They were gone. Alone in the quiet dark, I began to breathe again. Then, just as I was about to move, a silent white shape swooped down out of the black and landed not far from me. In the chinks of light that escaped through the slats of the sheds, I saw the heart-shaped face of a barn owl. It swivelled its head to stare at me and I held its eyes for a second. Then it swept back into the air with the body of a chick in its claws. I might not know exactly who was leaving them on Annie's doorstep, but at least the mystery of the Rowan House chicks had been solved. It was so simple. It was owls carrying the chicks to the hill. But seeing what went on at Lower Gillett had opened my eyes. Here was more proof of the suffering that we humans were causing by trying to increase productivity. Annie's words came echoing back to me, and at last I was beginning to understand them. 'Oh, Livia, nature's crying out. We've pushed her too hard, asked too much of her.'

Perhaps I should have felt guilty or scared, stupid or relieved as I cycled back from Lower Gillett Farm. But I didn't. I felt elated. I felt that same energy I'd felt on the hill, but this time I was in no doubt it was mine, it was flowing from me. I'd created it, by acting on my instincts. I felt stronger, braver, and after what I'd witnessed at the farm, defiant. I wasn't worried about Sadie. Something told me she would be alright. Her parents would give her a telling-off, but nothing major. And I had the photos. The first thing I did when I got in was send them to Sadie. Soon Oliver Jenkins' customers would know just how far from cheerful his chickens were.

In my bedroom, I met my own eyes in the mirror. They were shining behind a curtain of hair. No. Not right. My reflected image didn't match the new way I felt inside. Before I could change my mind, I fetched some scissors. My hair fell away in sheets. I cut it short beneath my ears and across my forehead in a blunt bob. 'No more hiding,' I promised myself hopefully as the last strands fell. I laughed out loud with exhilaration at the result. As I was changing out of my black clothes I noticed blood on my legs, between my thighs. Had I scratched myself without realising? Then it dawned on me: the scalding feeling in my stomach, the headache. My period had finally come. Through the curtains the moon sailed free from a bank of clouds into a limitless starry sky and I felt like I was sailing with her.

24 – Cast the Circle Thrice About

Sadie rang me the following day to let me know she was okay. But her voice was flat.

"You alright? What happened?"

"I'm fine. Just tired. I've just spent most of the night discussing animal welfare with that Jenkins man."

"The owner? Oh no. Was he furious? Sadie? You still there?"

Sadie eventually replied, sounding confused and miserable. "It's all legal, Liv. He showed me the certificate. Each hen is given a space a bit bigger than a piece of A4 paper. The leg burns, the light, the way he gets rid of the chicks. It's all legal."

"But if people could see …"

"Well, they will," Sadie announced defiantly. "Just because it's legal, it doesn't mean I'm not going to say anything. I've got the photos. I'm going to see the local papers today."

I set off for Annie's early to avoid Mum seeing what I'd done to my hair. I could only imagine what she'd say if she saw it. I left her a note saying, 'Staying at Sadie's tonight'. I wanted to put off going home for as long as possible.

It was a sparkling bright day. Celandines gleamed in the verges, and daffodils were out in the hedges, yellow trumpets on top of long stems that braced and shuddered in the chill

March wind. I picked Annie a bunch. I laughed to see the double take she did when she saw me.

"My goodness. I like the hair. Bit drastic, and needs a bit of levelling, but, all told, I think it suits you." She looked hard at me. "And there's something else, too, isn't there? What you looking so grown up for?" When I told her I'd started my period she cried out with excitement, hobbled towards me and squeezed my hand.

"It's a bit embarrassing," I muttered.

"Oh, don't let no one make you feel dirty or ashamed. It's the source of life, and something to be proud of. And on a full moon! Oh, this needs marking. The time has come at last." She held both my hands and looked at me. "Oh, my dear, I've been waiting for this moment. It's about time you learnt some secrets."

Annie sat me in front of her dressing table mirror to trim my hair. She layered my hair shorter and shorter still until all that remained was a boyish crop.

"You can take it. You got the cheekbones for it."

I ran my hand over my scalp. It felt amazing to be freed from my cloak of hair.

All day we worked hard together in the spring sunshine, sweeping the yard, mucking out the hen house. Later, Annie gave me a dressing gown and went to run me a bath while she made tea. She had placed a bag full of sprigs of rosemary under the tap, to bring luck, she said. If it was lucky or not, I couldn't tell but it smelled amazing. I stretched out in the water and relaxed after my long stressful night and my day of physical exercise. My back ached dully, but I welcomed the pain. It made me feel alive.

The light was fading. Annie picked up her stick and her bundle and hurried me out of the door and up the hill. I had never been on the hill at night-time, but with Annie for company I tingled with anticipation. Last night I had solved the riddle of the chicks, but the more I tried to fathom the secrets of the hill, the more they eluded me. Day by day, though, my senses were getting keener; I was learning a different way of seeing. Learning to trust my instincts made me alive to the signs all around me, the different energies I felt when I walked on the hill and in the woods.

Annie set down her bundle and laid a blanket at the base of Rowan House's northern wall, where the view of the hills, now pricked with light from outlying farms, spread before us. The North Star quavered in the indigo sky. I felt the chill breeze on my cheek and heard the rustle of the rowans. There was a pale glow on the eastern horizon. A white shape glided past before settling in a tree: a barn owl.

Annie took a deep breath and squeezed my hand. "I can't explain the magic here, Livia, no more than I can tell you how the world began. But look. Look to the skies and you'll see." She brushed her fingers lightly over my closing lids, and I felt the movement of the world turning, tipping us backwards into space.

I wasn't scared. I was ready for this – it felt like an initiation. I opened my eyes with a start and gasped; above me the planets wheeled, seasons passed, day and night came and went. The world righted itself and time began again, rolling through the years to tell the story of the hill, a procession of all who'd shared its power.

Way, way back in time, the first to come were swarthy people, dressed in furs and leather, carrying torches, carrying their babies on their backs. Fires glowed and lit up their rough faces. There were no rowan trees, instead, the whole hilltop was ringed by a stone circle. Figures weaved between tall boulders, capped with lintels. The figures began to dance. Limbs flailed to the sound of drums. Animals were brought in and blood was let in sacrifice; there was feasting. The fires flickered, the dancers faded and the world turned.

Now figures in robes filed up the hill, chanting; the lintels had fallen, but the piles of boulders were wreathed in spring flowers. Smiling men and women raised glinting cups to the bright sky before pairing off and disappearing into the surrounding woodland.

Firelight. A huge bonfire had been lit on Rowan Hill. To the east, an answering flame, on Pike Hill, and beyond and beyond, warning of invasion: the Spanish Armada. The flames died down and the hill was empty. It grew darker.

Rowan trees sprang from the mounds where the boulders had been and under the trees shadowy figures crept; their numbers were fewer and their faces hidden. I sensed fear and heard whispering. They had come to worship but now they must do it in secret. A dark moon followed; from the branches of each rowan swung the body of a worshipper accused of being a witch.

For a long time then the hill was empty. Then, finally, a lone woman came to the hill and gazed at the view. She wore a bonnet and full skirts that got in her way. Annie's grandmother. A man appeared and pulled her roughly away. I felt the stones at my back and knew then that the house, Rowan House, had been built on the sacred stones, the man's ruse to hide the purpose of the place. Rowan House crumbled again and Annie's mother came quietly, the sole guardian of the secret of the stones until her own daughter was old enough.

Then the sound of Annie's voice broke into my vision. Was what I'd seen just a story she'd told me? I was back in the here and now, rubbing my eyes and wondering.

"She is coming. Livia. Oh, but she's coming!"

25 – Wear the Blue Star On Your Brow

Creeping over the western horizon, as stately as a queen, the majestic moon climbed into the sky. She was veiled with an orange light, a dirty halo through which her face shone white.

"Oh," I sighed. I felt her pull me close, as if she drew at invisible strings connected to my heart and belly, strings that ran through my blood. It was a softer energy than that I'd felt on the hill. I bathed my face in the moonlight, unable to take my eyes from her beauty. Annie stood near me and raised her arms, drawing a wide arc over us. She raised up my hands until I felt I was cradling the moon. I felt her energy filling me like a cup, pouring into my outstretched hands in a gentle flow. Mellow moonlight filled each breath. My mind emptied and the knot in my belly melted away. I stood like that, totally at peace, until I was brim-full of light. The moon sailed slowly across the sky.

We walked back in silence, each with our own thoughts. My own were soft and marvelling. It was all too big and astonishing to try to make sense of. Annie seemed exhausted and a few times she stumbled. It had been cold on the hill, and the dew had made our clothes wet. I tucked her in with a hot water bottle as the pale light of dawn crept in. I took blankets downstairs, moved Nell from the couch and fell deeply and peacefully asleep.

I was woken by a knocking and a scrambling and barking of dogs. Annie appeared on the stairs looking rumpled and alarmed. She bent double to cough as she cowered in the stairwell. "Find out who it is, and tell 'em to go away," she pleaded.

I held Nell's collar firmly and undid the bolts. To my horror my mother stood in the doorway.

"Your hair!" she gasped, thrown for a moment. "So this is where you've been, all this time we thought you were at Sadie's. Sneaking about, creeping out of the house." Her voice was choked, half shouted, half sobbed. "We trusted you, Olivia. Where is she, your so-called friend, this Annie woman? I need to speak to her right now."

"You can't, Mum," I warned but Mum was already in the house, wading through the dogs and climbing the stairs.

"Mrs Tilke. Mrs Tilke! Are you here? Good God."

I caught up with her as she pushed into Annie's room. It was a state: damp pillars of mould climbed up the walls, and the paper was peeling off in one corner. The plaster sagged in places. Annie had wrapped herself in blankets and bolstered herself up against the bedstead. She looked terrified. Her eyes were wide and she looked a bit feverish to me.

"Mrs Tilke," Mum began, clearly shaken by what she saw, "I've come to get my daughter. I don't know if you were aware, but she didn't seek our permission before spending time with you so you'll understand if she doesn't come from now on." Mum looked around. "You shouldn't be living here alone, Mrs Tilke. You'd get a good price for this place, you know. You could move somewhere more manageable. I'm sure social services would be able to help. It's not right that a woman of your age should live in conditions like these. Olivia, get your things."

I searched wildly for Annie's help. Her face was downcast but she gave me a tiny nod.

"Olivia. Now!" ordered Mum.

I scurried after her, hating her with a passion. "How dare you barge into someone's house and be so rude. That was my friend you were talking to," I shouted as we marched out of the house.

"Your friend?" retorted Mum, turning on me. "Olivia, you are joking? I couldn't believe it when Sadie's mother rang and told me you weren't at their house. When she told me where you've been going all this time, do you know, I actually told her she must have made a mistake? You've made your father and I look complete fools." She held me by the arm. "You're not to come back here. Do you understand?"

"You can't forbid me. You don't own me," I shouted, shaking her off.

"I can't believe you're doing this to us, after everything this family has been through."

"I'm not doing anything to you."

"Olivia!" Mum cut me off. "As long as you live under my roof you will do as I say."

"I will not," I retorted, blind with rage. "I'd rather live with Annie. She knows me better than you ever will." That shut her up. She looked really hurt and I didn't care.

Slowly she spoke, in a small hurt voice. "I wouldn't let a child of mine stay one night in a house in that condition. If social services saw the state it's in, I'm sure that old woman would be moved out immediately. I wouldn't even keep a dog in those conditions."

"She's fine," I replied, realising too late the power Mum had to mess everything up. "Please, Mum," I begged, "you mustn't contact social services. She'd die if she had to move."

"I'll have to think about that, Olivia. After all, someone should be considering what's best for that old woman."

"Mum, please. She hasn't done anything wrong. Just leave her be," I pleaded.

My mother ran her hand through her hair and let out a shaky breath. "Oh, Olivia, haven't you heard what they say about her? I can't tell you how worried I was when I heard you were up here. It's common knowledge in the village what that woman did."

I gave my mother a confused look.

"What? You mean you don't know?"

Oh no. I didn't want to find out like this. I turned my head away, hardening myself to what she might say.

"They say she killed someone, Olivia. Poisoned a young woman, and her baby too."

Above our heads Annie's bedroom window shut with a thud.

26 – Heed the North Wind's Mighty Gale

"I'm so sorry, Liv. I was trying to cover for you," Sadie wailed. "Mum thought you were involved in the break-in at the chicken farm, and I said you weren't, and that you wouldn't get involved because Jack was a friend of Annie's and then she asked who Annie was and I hate lying to my mum and she'd been so cool about the break-in. I'm really sorry. I've completely ballsed it up for you, haven't I?"

I forgave her. But I wasn't allowed to see her outside of school until after exams. I thought of all the plans we'd made for summer and wondered if they would ever happen now. According to my parents, Sadie was now a bad influence. Her face had been in all the local papers. 'Local girl reveals truth behind Cheerful Chickens'; 'Teen uncovers barn eggs scandal' and 'Shocking cost of cheap eggs'.

There had been lots of astonished and upset letters to the paper, letters demanding the brand name Cheerful Chickens be scrapped, calls for changes in the law. Sadie was pleased. "Consumer influence. If no one buys them, he'll be forced to make things better for the chickens. I'm on a mission, Liv."

I missed Annie. I missed the dogs. I couldn't afford to see my friend for a bit, but I rang her several times a day. I told her I was being watched, that I couldn't come, but I don't know if she believed me. She sounded guarded, and I couldn't think what to talk about.

"Is it true what Mum said?" I wanted to cry. "Tell me it's not true." Every time it rained, I thought of her, ill and alone in that damp house.

Easter came and went. My mother escorted me to the bus stop in the morning and met me at the bus stop on the way home. She had Mrs Enticott ring her when I arrived and left on a Saturday, and she timed my bike ride home. I worked alongside Robert and tuned in with his simmering rage. Neither of us were free to be ourselves, to decide our own fates. But I couldn't talk to him about Annie. He was as bad as all the others when it came to her.

Perhaps I should have felt sorry for my mother; God knows she had enough to deal with without me giving her grief, but I festered with hate for her, and that was the extra motivation I needed to do well in my exams. I knuckled down to my revision. I would show her, leave no shadow of a doubt that I could do it. I was going to be my own person, not her clone. I sat up late at night studying, until I knew the syllabus for each exam back to front and inside out. Sometimes, as I stared out of my window at the clouds scudding across the moon, I opened the drawer next to my bed and took out the length of frayed red thread that Annie had given me. I wrapped it around my finger and thought I could hear the voice from the hilltop, whispering encouragement to me. It was probably just my imagination, but I so needed to believe that the voice was real. I waited. I waited for my chance to slip away.

It came one night in late April. April showers had spattered all month, and on that particular day, all day, a strong wind had been brewing. The classroom windows rattled, and there was talk of gales. On the way home the high-sided school bus rocked and the little kids squealed with excitement. When I got to the bus stop, there was no one there to meet me. I got a call on my mobile. It was Dad.

"Now before I say anything else, we're alright, that's the main thing, no one hurt, but we came back to find the car had been hit by a fallen tree. We're at the garage. It could take a few hours. Now you're to stay at home, you hear. We'll ring you when we're on our way."

It didn't occur to me to be worried about them in the gales. This was my chance. I ran all the way to Annie's, wishing the high wind would pick me up and carry me there.

The rain stung my face as I beat on the door. "Annie, Annie. It's me," I cried. The wind wailed; could I hear footsteps? I heard nothing. "Annie!" There was a light on in the sitting room. I knew she was at home. "Annie," I called one last time. It was then I heard the tiny, choked noise of someone crying. I knelt by the letterbox. "Let me in, Annie," I pleaded.

The latch opened. She looked so shrunken standing there, her eyes pink. I rushed to hug her as an explosion of dogs broke free from the sitting room and we tumbled laughing and crying into the house.

"I thought you'd had it with me," Annie confided as she blew her nose. "Thought you was just like all the others."

"But I rang you. I told you I couldn't come."

"It sounded like excuses. Couldn't you have come to see me?"

"If I could have, I would have sneaked out. But I'm being watched all the time, I told you. If my mum knew I was here."

I clutched my mobile phone. Even though I knew there was no reception downstairs in her kitchen, I needed to check it wasn't transmitting my conversation to my mother. "I hate her."

"Don't say that. Hate will only bring you harm."

"I know, but it's true. Annie, what am I going to do?"

An awkward silence fell. Annie got up, went to a cupboard and took down her silver bowl. She filled it with water from a jug and lit candles. She turned off the lights. "When I can't see the way forward, sometimes this helps. It's called scrying. Will you try it?"

I nodded. That strange old bowl had always fascinated me, with its mysterious carvings. Though I wasn't really expecting to see anything in the bowl, I wanted to look, and I so wanted to know.

"Then first you need to clear your mind."

The surface of the water glinted silver. I tried to empty my mind, but all I could hear was my mother's mocking 'Do you mean you don't know?'

I looked up into Annie's eyes. "What happened, Annie? Will you tell me the truth?"

A look of panic crossed her face, and her hand went to her mouth. She squeezed her eyes tight shut and gestured to the bowl. Slowly, quietly, she began to speak. Was it my imagination, or did I glimpse something in the dark waters?

At first, I thought it was a reflection from the candle, a flicker of light, but as I looked more closely the room seemed to darken and fade out of focus as her words took shape in the ripples. It was not candlelight but snow – a quiet, suffocating snow that flitted across the surface of the water, piling into drifts. Snow like I'd never seen in my lifetime, even in the coldest winter. There was no sound, the snow seemed to have muffled that. Looming out of the white, a woman. Her skin like the snow, and her hair pale. She was crouching in the corner of her bedroom. Her belly stuck out between her knees, firm and round; she was heavily pregnant. The woman's face was wild with agony, her hair plastered to her with sweat. I could not hear the sound of her screams but I knew she was begging for help. Annie was there supporting her, a younger, red-haired Annie, smoothing her brow, whispering words of encouragement, and then the woman would smile, the contraction over. She would move about, rolling her hips and rubbing her back. Annie gave the woman tea, made from herbs she carried in her pouch.

In the corridor, the father paced. He was not to be allowed in. He dared not go in. Another woman, the man's younger sister by the look of her, brought hot towels. Her brown eyes were wild with the shock of witnessing her first birth. She was dark, neat black hair, a snub nose and defensive, pursed lips. She went to the window and shook her head. The ambulance could not get through.

Downstairs the woman's older children, girls, all of them, glanced up at the ceiling. The younger ones whimpered. Grandmother took them to bed. Another contraction was building; the two women held the labouring mother on either side as she wailed to the heavens and asked for release. The hours passed. The woman squatted on the floor, her arms and head resting on the bed. Her fingers clawed at the bed sheets as Annie massaged her back, but when it was over, she did not smile. The man sat with his back to the door, his head in his hands. Annie offered her more tea, but the woman could not drink it. Annie's face was tense, and the younger woman sniffled. Annie had the woman climb onto the bed. The baby's head was visible, a crown of dark hair; Annie praised the mother, told her to push, took the baby by the shoulders and pulled it out. It was a boy. I saw steam in the cold air as the blood flowed out after the limp, dark body.

Annie clamped the baby's cord, sucked the baby's nostrils and began to rub it with a towel. The young woman who had been smiling now started screaming. The father burst in just as his wife started to fit, shaking and jerking, all the while pumping red blood onto the bed. All the pushing must have made her haemorrhage. He sank to his knees at the sight of the blood. The woman became still. Annie thrust the baby into the young woman's arms and she took over the rubbing while Annie tried to find his mother's pulse. She climbed onto the bed, pumping the woman's chest and trying to massage some life back into her. It was futile. The woman's eyes were open but she never saw her son. The baby never drew breath. I had my answer. Blood seeped into the scrying bowl, tinging the water pink.

"I'm glad you know now. I'm sorry you had to see it, though," Annie told me, taking my trembling hand. Her eyes were wide and desolate, as if she had been reliving what I'd seen.

"You gave her something to drink, Annie. What was it?" I asked shakily.

"Raspberry leaf, blue cohosh, motherwort. To help with the contractions. I never gave Rose Tremayne no poison."

"Tremayne! That's why those men were staring at me." I told her about the men at the New Year's party.

"Nephews. The father, Roy, he remarried and moved away a few years after. It was him that started it, about the poison. It was the grief made him say it I suppose. He'd lost his wife and son. The children had lost their mother. And there's me, couldn't have no children of my own. I suppose he thought I was jealous. That I couldn't bear to see her so blessed with children when I couldn't manage one. He wanted someone to blame. Couldn't blame the snow, the cord round the baby's neck." Annie lips were pursed tight. "And all these years, I've took the blame. I never asked for no sympathy. I never minded giving up the company of those village gossips. Ted stood by me. May, that's Jack's mother, she stood by me. Then they passed on and I got used to being on my own. I got my animals. I hadn't got no more to lose in the way of friendship. Till I met you."

Annie bit her lip, but it was too late. A tear spilled and splashed on the table. "Oh, say you don't blame me, Liv. Say you believe me. I couldn't bear to lose you too."

I took her frail body in my arms and hugged her. "I believe you, Annie," I said.

She laughed ruefully. "Perhaps I'm lucky. My neighbours only turned their backs on me. Time was, they would have burnt me, or hung me from the nearest tree."

Soon my parents would be on their way back. I had to get home. But my resolve was set.

"I'll never leave you again, Annie. I promise."

Summer

Summer

27 – When Ye Have and Hold a Need

It was June. With all my hours of study and revision my exams were a breeze. I was pretty sure I'd done well, and, although officially I was still forbidden from seeing Annie, I felt freer. I'd been finding ways to see her. I cycled to the Enticott's along hedgerows bursting with wild flowers. The hedges crowded closer, nature reached out. Trees touched their branches overhead; the latticework of leaves looked like fingers interlocking against a backdrop of blue sky. It had rained earlier and the puddles floated with a scurf of elderflowers; heavy heads of bruised blossom hung from the trees, giving off a nasty-sweet perfume. I thought of the wine Sadie and I had planned to make, the trips to the River Dart. They hadn't happened and they probably wouldn't now. I'd been busy at the dairy farm and Annie's. Sadie had found a summer job picking fruit. On top of that she had met this boy called Matt and was happily absorbed by being in love. I missed my friend but I was doing alright by myself.

June was full of promise; it was there in the tiny white flowers of the wild strawberry plants, in the dog roses that would fall in autumn from ripening rosehips and the pale pink bramble flowers that would fatten into blackberries. The air was sweet with earth smells, and in the fields each blade of grass

159

held a rainbow drop of water that would soon evaporate towards the warming sun. The birds babbled. The swallows who'd arrived from Africa two months ago were slicing through the air, twisting and swooping for gnats to feed their chicks.

The farmyard was strangely empty when I arrived. Mr Enticott's Land Rover had gone and the farm dogs were quiet. The cows had been milked already and Robert was sluicing out the dairy.

"Could 'a done with you earlier today," he snapped. "Mum and Dad've taken the bullocks to market and a cow's come down with milk fever. My stupid fool father don't switch his mobile on. Can't afford to get the vet out unless we have to, and I'm not making that call without his say-so. Come and take a look."

I heard the cow before I saw her – with each breath she exhaled a painful-sounding lowing. She staggered backwards when we entered.

"It's the early stages, her legs are weak and her temperature low."

"But what's caused it?"

"She ain't got enough calcium. All the milking takes it out of 'em. The vet would give her a shot of it but vets' bill ain't cheap. She's a good milker, but an older cow. Most likely Dad'd just let her go rather than pay."

I must have given him a look, because he retorted, "He ain't hard-hearted, Liv. Things are that tight at the moment. If she's in pain, he'd put her out o' her misery."

"Shoot her?"

He nodded. As if she had understood, the cow buckled at the knees and sank to the ground.

"Bloody hell. Liv, get in the pen," Robert shouted. I vaulted over the fence just in time to deflect the bale of straw that he fairly threw at me. "Get it behind her. We've got to stop her lying flat out. She mustn't get her head down or her heart'll fail."

He threw more bales at me as I built a kind of wall behind the cow, hemming her in and keeping her head up. She stopped lowing but instead began to twist her head back towards her body as if trying to locate the source of pain. It was a rhythmic lunge that was beyond her control.

"You poor thing," I whispered. "You gave all that milk and now it's made you sick. Isn't there something we can do?" I fretted, crouching by the pen and listening to her laboured breathing

"You got any brilliant suggestions?" Robert snapped.

The cow shivered. Her eyes were dull and her nose was dry. Suddenly she mooed wildly, tipped her head back and tried to rest it on a ledge of straw bales. I could hardly bear to watch. "She's in agony," I told Robert. "Wouldn't it be kinder to let her lie down. Let her go?"

I could see from his anxious face that he felt for the animal. I thought for a minute he might accept my suggestion. But, instead, he grabbed a handful of his own hair and shook his head. "I've seen them take hours to die. It's no kinder. And I'm not shooting her without Dad's say-so. So we've got to try to get her through this. I just – I just can't think what to do." He was pacing now.

Then I realised. "Annie can help."

"Annie Tilke?" he barked sarcastically. "What's she gonna do, fly over here on her broomstick and sacrifice a cockerel?"

"Do you enjoy being ignorant?" I hissed. "What d'you think people did before vets? What did your grandfather do when he couldn't afford the vet's bills? Annie knows more about animals than anyone I know. You're just too proud to accept help from an old woman."

"No, I ain't," he retorted, looking stung. "Doubt she'd come anyway. More likely try to poison it from what I've heard." It came out of his mouth before he had a chance to check himself.

"You don't believe that story any more than I do," I told him disdainfully.

He looked sheepish. "So you know then. Who told you?"

"Annie did. What *really* happened, and I believe her, but I don't suppose the truth is as interesting as village gossip. Oh well, let's just sit here and watch this animal die, shall we?"

Robert was in trouble. He returned to sitting on his haunches, stroking the cow's flank as she heaved. He tried his dad's mobile again. "How's she gonna get here?" he asked irritably.

"You'll have to get her in the tractor. You can get to hers across the fields, can't you?"

"What if she won't come?"

"Then she won't come. We won't know unless we ask her, will we?"

Actually, I couldn't think of one reason why Annie *would* agree to come. In all the time I'd known her she'd never left her few acres of land. Now I knew the accusation made against her I could understand why she never went out. For the last thirty years her own community had virtually shut its doors to her.

"Don't do no harm to ask, I suppose. We don't tell Dad, though, agreed? I'll never live it down if he thinks his cows has had spells done on 'em."

I called Annie on my mobile. I pictured the phone ringing in Annie's living room – it was an old Bakelite thing with a twirly dial. Annie would be in the still room or busy with the goats. She didn't always hear the phone when it rang.

It took me three phone calls and ten minutes of explaining and cajoling to persuade her. At first she hung up on me. She was angry with me and embarrassed. As I explained the cow's symptoms and distress she began to listen. I suggested some herbs but I didn't know what I was talking about.

"No, no, that wouldn't do no good at all, water mint and nettles would have prevented all this but it's too late for that now. No matter anyway, I ain't coming."

In the end I got Robert to speak to her. He stood stiff as a statue holding the phone, the other arm tight across his chest as if protecting himself from some black magic that might slip down the phone line into his ear. But he explained the symptoms and she confirmed his diagnosis.

Businesslike, he rang off. "She says I should pick her up directly. She says she needs two pounds of molasses, a bucket of warm water and a boiled kettle. Molasses is in the shed. When you got all the other stuff you better stay with the cow, case anything happens."

I wasn't sure if he meant to him or the animal.

I ran to the shed and prepared the ingredients. Then I went back to the cow. I dreaded her dying in agony before they got back. I spoke quietly to her, willing her to pull through. But before my eyes she was fading. She wasn't going to last much longer. Her eyes were looking glazed and her breath was raspy and laboured.

"What should I do? What should I do?" I said to no one, wringing my hands and pacing round the cow shed.

Before long I heard the sound of the tractor approaching. They made a strange sight, the pair of them. Robert was thin-lipped, staring out front, with Annie bundled up behind him, perching on the frame of the cab. She was carrying a bag in which I assumed were her herbs. I wondered if they'd exchanged any words at all on the journey.

"She looks bad," Annie said, tutting. "The milk fever can take 'em quick so we'd best get started." She set to work quickly, talking quietly to the cow as she did so.

"Alright m'dear, we'll have you right in no time. We're gonna make you a drench that'll sort you out. Robert, pour the molasses into the bucket of water and mix it, please," she instructed in the same sing-song voice.

He did as he was told.

"That's the calcium she needs." She reached into the bag and added two handfuls of a brownish powder to the drench. "Powdered seaweed. Full of iodine. Now we gotta get it down her."

With the last of her strength the cow thrashed against Robert as he tried to hold her head still. I was afraid she'd knock him out with her bony skull. We were all covered in the dark, malty liquid. Annie and I used a funnel and a tube to pour the drench into the cow and the brown medicine disappeared down her throat.

"What now?" panted Robert.

"Now we wait," Annie replied.

Annie talked to the cow in a low voice, saying things we could not hear. The cow's great hairy ear twitched from time to time. Robert looked anxious. But after half an hour, the cow lifted her head up by herself. Robert was speechless. Annie's voice grew animated – she praised the cow and stroked her bony spine and flanks. After three quarters of an hour, the cow tried to stand.

"Not yet, m'dear. You rest up. Let's drench her again and then leave her be. She's on the mend. Keep your eyes out for mastitis. If you see any signs, get a calf back on her for a bit."

We were all sticky with molasses and covered in straw and cow hair when we emerged into the midday sun. Annie looked around the farmyard, curious after all these years to see into someone else's life.

"Shall I show you around?" Robert offered.

Annie's eyes were bright and tiny pinpricks of pink glowed in her cheeks. She nodded and followed him for a tour of the farm. I let myself into the farmhouse and made us all strong cups of tea.

"Over Heydon way they milk Holsteins," Robert was telling her when they returned. "Blooming great things, milk yield's good but their feet go after a couple of years. Terrible to see 'em staggering lame up the ramp to slaughter."

"There's always a price to pay when you push Nature too hard," Annie agreed.

"You're right there. Thank you for what you did today, Mrs Tilke."

"Call me Annie," she chastised as I handed out the tea.

Later, Annie sat resting on a hay bale waiting for Robert to give her a lift back home. He was helping me take in the tea things. In the cool of the kitchen, he turned to me and his warm brown eyes met mine for a second. Slowly he ran one calloused finger up my bare arm. His touch was electrifying. My skin prickled and all the tiny hairs stood up.

"Thanks, Liv. I couldn't have done that without you," he said.

I held my breath, willing him to stay, willing him to touch me again. But he just chuckled, threw the tractor keys in the air, caught them and left the house. I grinned all the way home, still tingling from his touch.

The cow made a full recovery. Nobody said a word about Annie, and Mr Enticott was impressed at his son's quick thinking in drenching the cow. It had saved both money on vet's bills and a good milker's life. It brought a brief spell of peace between father and son. In the weeks that followed, Robert and I worked side by side in the dairy. Before we let the cows out to pasture, I helped vaccinate them against bluetongue and leptospirosis and I was allowed to help with calving too. It was me who pulled on the calf's forelegs, all the while calling my encouragement to the cow. It was me who cleared the calf's nostrils with straw, then watched the miracle of it tottering to its feet, still wet, to find its mother's udder.

I was proving I had the makings of a vet and, maybe, a healer too, someone who went outside the medicine books to soothe and mend. I was getting stronger, inside and out. I could feel the muscles flex in my upper arms as I lugged bales of straw or carried buckets of water. My short hair was getting blonde highlights in the sun, and, on Mrs Enticott's huge breakfasts, I was filling out. Sometimes, when we worked together, I thought I saw Robert's beautiful brown eyes linger on me just a bit longer than they used to, but I was probably imagining it. Nonetheless, with all the physical exercise I was getting I even slept well, though Dad was no better at nights. It felt like the glorious summer would stretch on and on, as if it would never end. I should have known it was too good to be true.

It was the calm before the storm.

28 – Hearken Not to Others' Greed

I found the heron's skull at the top of the hill, in the middle of the rowan circle. It had been propped up with splints made of the bird's leg bones. Both bones had been pushed down into the soil, and one had stuck into the heron's skull, while the other had been crushed and split to make a crutch for the long, heavy beak. Fragments of flesh still stuck to the skull, along with a few grey feathers. Annie had told me about curses like these, not that she'd ever have used such a thing. Without touching the hideous object, I followed the angle of the beak with my eyes. It had been set to point at the object of its curse: Annie's cottage. I kicked it hard and the bones scattered apart. This was no practical joke. Whoever had done this was deliberate, nasty and full of real hatred. It was horrible to think they had set foot on the hill.

I felt unsteady on my feet as I descended to the cottage. Should I tell Annie? Was the power in the curse itself, or just in knowing you'd been cursed?

Robert was up on the roof. It was his way of thanking Annie for her help. I was suddenly shy to see him with his shirt off; he shone brown in the sun and the muscles in his back flexed as he reached to nail down some roofing felt.

"There's a few tiles gone, but I've got spares at the farm. If this weather lasts the house'll dry out and my patching will keep it that way."

I smiled. Together we'd been sorting the house out for Annie, chopping some wood, scrubbing at the mould. If Mum did call social services, they'd find nothing out of order.

"Least I could do," Robert declared, stretching. "What she did for that cow, I tell you, I learnt something, that day."

I decided I would tell Annie about the curse. I never could keep things from her anyway.

"A heron's skull. That's their way of reminding me I'm a witch again, I suppose," she muttered when I told her what I'd found.

"It didn't look like something someone in the village would dream up though."

"Oh, any old book'll tell you how to lay a curse. Fingernail clippings, pins in a beeswax poppet, all that nasty nonsense. Don't you fret. I've protection charms to match ill will." She pointed to the bottles on the sill. They were small comfort to me, though I was glad Annie wasn't worried.

"I'm glad you've got the dogs." I shivered, thinking of her alone in the house at night.

"Oh, Nell'd protect me to the death, I'm sure of that," Annie breezed, as Nell butted her hand with a wet nose. "If someone's trying to scare me away, they'll have to try harder than that. You'll stay for lunch?" she asked, ushering me in.

The smell of roast chicken wafted from the range. The dogs gazed lovingly at Annie, dreaming of giblets.

I set the table, picked sweet peas from Annie's garden and set them in the centre. Awkwardly, Robert let himself in. He'd pulled a white shirt on over his bare chest, but the buttons had come undone at the neck. There was no point denying it to myself, I really fancied him. And perhaps more importantly, I was starting to like him. I looked down at my lap for fear my face would give my churning feelings away.

"I've done what I can. It'll hold out the winter at any rate, and it shouldn't be so damp."

"You're a good boy. You must take some jars of jam for your mother," said Annie.

Robert looked alarmed. His parents had no idea he was here.

"Now, shall we eat?"

Annie had made creamy mashed potatoes and fresh peas in their pods to go with the chicken. She carved the bird, one of her own, plucked that morning, and we tucked into the delicious meal. Annie asked Robert for news of all the local farming families and he did his best to update her.

"Mr Kibby? No, he moved away years back. The Keens live there now, they got two young kids at the school, moved from over Axminster way. Mrs Keen, she used to be a Phillips, you know, old Mr Phillips? He had a stroke and he's in a home in Seaton now."

Their world was so tightly woven, so intricately connected. I could see how the threads still tugged Annie, though she'd been cut off so long.

"And you're the eldest, ain't you, Robert?" confirmed Annie. "You carrying on with your education or will you be taking over the running of the farm?"

Robert's face grew dark. "I dunno."

"What's that meant to mean?"

"It means I don't know what's going to happen. We're a small family farm, we breed our own stock. We're small enough that we have time for the animals, we know 'em, so we know if they're off colour. But we don't make no money. Bottom line – we survive. And it seems like that's not good enough no more. Not to Dad, anyway."

"Nobody never said farming would make you rich. 'Tisn't all about making money, Robert."

"Don't I know it." He grimaced.

"There are those round here that would bleed the land dry, exploit the livestock with never a thought for their welfare, all for a quick profit. You're keeping up the traditions that make the countryside what it is, holding the land for future generations. You should feel proud of being a farmer."

"I am, I am. When I turn the cows out to grass in the spring, and watch them galloping about, or when we get the hay stacked up in the barn ready for winter, then I feel proud. But to tell you the truth, I reckon my dad's got to me. Most of the time recently, Mrs Tilke, I can't help thinking I'm a right mug."

"Pah. What d'you mean by that?" asked Annie dismissively, but Robert had a point to make.

"Getting up at five a.m. in the dark to walk across some freezing field to pull a sheep out of a hedge. Or getting up at dawn then racing around till midnight silaging 'cos the weather's gonna change. If I charged by the hour, d'you know what I could make? Seems like it's alright for everyone else to put their prices up – the vets, the feed merchants – but if us farmers try to charge more for our milk then the supermarkets go ballistic, the customers dig their heels in, and we're back where we started." He hesitated, looking almost guilty. He nodded at me. "Last week I went to see that Mr Tremayne's pig farm, the one Dad was talking about."

I stared at him in disbelief. How could he even say that name in her house? Had he forgotten Annie's history with that family? Annie herself looked uncomfortable.

He'd touched a nerve but Robert carried on, unthinking. "It's another world, I tell you. I ain't never seen a farm like it. More like a factory really. He's minting it. He never has to get his hands dirty, hardly has to get out of bed to see to those pigs. All their needs, the computer deals with. They finish their food, there's a sensor, and more food comes down the chute. They have sprinklers that wash the slurry out of an evening. Oh, I know they're all on antibiotics and shut in all day, but I dunno, I thought maybe those pigs would be suffering."

"You mean they weren't?" Annie asked through pursed lips.

"I thought you said they got so bored in those places they went cannibal?" I reminded him. This conversation was going dangerously astray.

"Maybe they do. I didn't ask. I didn't see none of that when I was there. Most of them were in metal pens, separated."

Annie let out a little 'oh' of shock.

"Look, perhaps they weren't as happy as a pig troughing about in the mud, but they were clean, well-fed, warm. Perhaps it's not much of a life, but they looked alright to me," he conceded, unable to meet our eyes.

"What did you visit the farm for, Robert?" Annie asked perceptively.

Robert squared his shoulders. "Dad asked me to. He wanted me to have a look. Reckon going over to pigs might be an option when I take over the farm."

"You said yourself, those pigs don't have any kind of life," I said sharply, unable to keep my disappointment from my voice. "They're just so much pork. And it's as much your farm as it is your dad's."

"I know that. That's why I've got to decide what we're going to do. We can't afford to carry on like we are," he snapped back. "We gotta live. My back's against the wall. I know lots of farmers feel the same way. Lots of 'em are going over to these High Health pigs."

"Then maybe they don't deserve to call themselves farmers no more," burst out Annie.

Robert stood up, his dark face flushed and scowling. He pulled back his chair, scraping it across the tiles. "Well, lucky for me I don't need your permission, Mrs Tilke. Or yours, Olivia. And maybe I don't want to spend the rest of my life shovelling …" He bit his tongue because of Annie's age. "Shovelling muck!" And with that he turned and marched out of the house.

We sat in silence, looking at our laps. I was embarrassed by him.

After a while Annie spoke. "That time at the Enticott's, when I helped with the cow, I suppose I got me hopes up. 'Bout the next generation of farmers." She shook her head and sighed as she retreated sadly upstairs for a lie down. Just when I'd begun to think I could respect him, Robert had dashed both our hopes. Furious and disappointed, I cleared away the remains of our ruined meal.

29 – Three Times Bad

I dreamt of the rotting heron's skull. I was penned in, in a metal cage like the pigs Robert told us about. I couldn't move, I was trapped and I felt it coming for me, slowly, probing, with its beak near my ear. When I woke, my breath came in short, hard gasps. I heard shouting and I couldn't work out if it was coming from me. On the landing there was a thud as my mother stumbled on a step, lights were switched on and the shouting stopped. I was only shouting silently. It was my father who had once more woken the house with his agony.

I was still shaky and irritable when I got to the Enticotts' farm later that morning. It was a week since I had last been. I was angry with Robert for the way he'd spoken to Annie, and now I held him responsible for the dream too. I spotted his blue boiler suit inside the bonnet of a knackered old tractor. Robert's dad hadn't been able to afford the shiny new tractor he wanted yet. I braced myself. It was about time someone stood up to Robert's rudeness.

"Don't you think you should be ashamed?" I accused him. But it wasn't Robert fixing the engine. It was Wadsy.

"Flippin' 'eck, Liv. What have I done now? I only just got 'ere and already you're having a go at me."

"What are you doing here?" I fumbled.

"Pleased to see you too. Robsy got me a job. Bloody brilliant, innit? Dad kicked me out when school finished and I been dossing about staying with friends 'n' that. I rang Robsy and he said they could do with another pair of hands here, so I'm sorted. Mrs Enticott's feeding me up, I even got a place to stay in one o' the old bungalows. And I get to work with you, eh Liv?" He leered. "Nice one, eh?"

I couldn't believe Robert would offer Wadsy a job. He knew about Wadsy's crush on me and must have worked out by now I seriously wasn't interested. Having Wadsy around would spoil everything. Of all the petty things to do. He must really want rid of me. Perhaps I was too much like a guilty conscience to be around while he ploughed on with his plans for the pig farm. Well, if Robert really wanted rid of me, I would stop coming. I had done enough work experience to put on my CV. We need never see each other again.

"Where is Robert, anyway?" I muttered.

"Ain't that the million-dollar question. No one knows. He's had another set-to with his dad and gone AWOL. Mr Enticott said he ain't been home, ain't slept in his bed this week. That's why I started work straightaway. Man, I don't wanna be in Robsy's shoes when he comes home."

The cows must have sensed my mood because one aimed a kick at me as I tried to wash her for milking. Her hoof glanced off my shoulder, but I was left with a purple bruise and a stiff neck. Over lunch I saw that Wadsy already had his feet under the table.

"Another helping, Richard?" Mrs Enticott insisted, spooning more cottage pie onto his plate. "Needs eating. Will only go to waste otherwise."

Wadsy was already becoming a substitute son and he lapped up the attention. "Lovely job, Mrs Enticott. You're a brilliant cook, you are. You should sell some o' your stuff down the farmers' market. You'd make a killing!"

It was hard to begrudge him a bit of motherly fussing. I doubt he got much at home. Like a stray dog brought in from the cold, he'd repay those crumbs of affection with slavering loyalty.

I set off up Annie's lane. She was waiting for me in her doorway. Her white hair was wild and her papery hands fluttered about her face.

"It's Nell. She's missing. Never came in last night. I've looked and looked. Liv, I don't know what to do."

Cold dread washed through me. Kind Nell, Nell the protector. She would never leave Annie.

"I expect she's gone off rabbiting and got lost," I reassured Annie. "Or maybe she's found a boyfriend in the village. Have you rung the police to see if they've found any lost dogs?"

She had and they hadn't. But we couldn't rest until we'd searched everywhere again. We left Pip and Noggin shut in the house. I noticed Annie had started locking her back door.

"Nell. Nell!" we called. At any moment I expected to see her long, lollopy form galloping down the hill to us. She would leap up, planting her fore-paws on my chest, and cover me with kisses, her bearded face tickling mine. She would jump down and let me caress her ears with my fingertips; her ears were the softest thing I'd ever felt. Then she would charge off and cavort in ever-widening circles with a silly grin on her face. We mounted the hill.

"Nell. Come on. Good dog!"

Our voices grew shrill. She'd be in such trouble when we found her.

"Blummin' dog. Got us traipsing up hill and down dale. Probably be there waiting for us, happy as Larry, when we get back."

We had reached the rowans and walked in silence to Rowan House. My nerves jangled with every step and by the time we reached the hummocks under the trees we were both stumbling, half jogging, praying that our dread would soon turn to relief.

As we rounded the fallen side of the hilltop ruin, we found Nell. She was lying in the shelter of one of the walls, stretched out flat. She could have been asleep but for the flecks of blood and foam at her mouth and nose. Annie uttered a hoarse cry and fell to her knees. She heaved raw sobs as she crawled towards her friend. She leant her head close to Nell's stiff ears and caressed her unresponsive face. I felt my own knees buckle.

"No, no, no, no, no," was all either of us could manage to say. This was the worst of our imaginings. I knelt next to Nell and ran my hand over her wiry fur. Her body was cold and hard under my hand, the way I felt inside. She had been dead for many hours.

Eventually, we wrapped Nell in our coats and carried her down the hill. We took her inside and laid her body by the range as if by some miracle the warmth might revive her. Pippin skittered towards her expectantly, before stopping sharply and retreating anxiously to his bed. Noggin solemnly sniffed her all over, before lying near her head with his chin on his paws.

"'Twas a custom in these parts to tell the bees when there was a death in the house. To dress the hives in black. But even the bees have gone."

"Annie. I think it's time to call the police," I said.

"What for?" Annie sniffed.

"Whoever did this, they really want to hurt you. This is really serious."

"Olivia. I told you before, I don't wanna get the police involved."

"Why not?"

"I don't want people sniffing about. Thinking I can't manage. Putting me away, for my own good."

"But what if they come back? What next?"

"Look, who's to say it weren't an accident? Most likely she went off ratting in someone's shed and ate some rat poison. It has all the signs of rat poison."

"But the nearest farm's a mile away," I protested, "and Nell never went far from the house. She didn't want to leave you."

"I know you want someone to blame. But for all I've been teased and baited, I just can't believe that anyone would poison my Nell. I don't want to believe that of people. The day I start thinking like that is the day I lose my faith in the goodness of this world. I'm sorry, Liv."

Annie might not believe in the devil, but, nonetheless, evil had crept into our lives, and taken poor Nell from us. And, without her faithful protector, Annie was left old and weak and vulnerable. Without Annie to guide me, how would I find my way? The thought terrified me.

30 – Nine Woods in the Cauldron Go

Midsummer's Eve. The night before the longest day of the year. Mum was in London visiting Amber, and Dad never much noticed where I was. I planned to stay out all night. A warm breeze skimmed our skin as we built the bonfire inside the walls of Rowan House and, although it was growing late, the sun had not sunk beneath the horizon. The undersides of the rowan leaves fluttered silver in the evening light. It was meant to be a time of celebration, but since Nell's death I had felt numb with grief. All her joy, her open love, her honesty seemed to have left our lives when she did. She was buried amongst the rose bushes, but I still expected her to greet me every day.

I could not accept Annie's theory that it was an accident. Something had changed on the hill. Before, when I lay inside the circle of rowans, I'd been so sure I could feel them giving off some kind of energy. But I couldn't feel the charge from the stones anymore. I could not lie on the earth without remembering that Nell had suffered her terrible death there. Perhaps it was my own flatness I was recognising, or, if it were true and there really was a special charge coming from the stones, perhaps my sadness was stopping me feeling it. Could it be that someone else knew the hill's secret? That they were draining the power from the stones for their own nasty purposes? Someone threatening, someone that wanted to harm Annie, who had been shadowing her for years, and was now drawing closer?

Before we'd left Annie's cottage, I'd done a bad thing. I'd crept to the still room and taken a handful of henbane seeds from one of the high jars. I'd researched it on the internet. It affected the brain and heart. Too much could cause a fast heartbeat, dizziness. The leaves were poison, but the smoke from the seeds, inhaled, had other properties. Annie's book said the Greeks had used it to give second sight. I needed that sight. I needed to know who'd killed Nell.

As it approached its zenith, summer edged closer to winter. Annie herself looked older, hunched and defeated by life. She barely lifted her eyes from the ground. I thought back to the day she had wrapped the red thread around my wrist, and it seemed so long ago. 'Courage,' she had said. I had found such strength in her faith. Now I found it hard to believe in anyone or anything. The thought even crossed my mind, perhaps Annie *would* be safer in a home. 'For her own good.' I felt instantly ashamed, and heaved another branch onto the stack. The nine kinds of wood we used in the fire were special ones. Birch wood was meant to block evil spirits, oak had the power of protection. Fir and vine gave second sight ... Another *need fire*, another plea for help. It all felt like a waste of time.

The sun was sinking into a bank of gauzy clouds. On the western horizon, the sky was tinged with pink and violet. Tiny clouds still caught the sun's rays, their undersides flecked with orange. And then, at last, the sun was gone. The colours dimmed and a cool breeze blew in from the sea. Slowly, like a shy guest taking her place at the party, a pale moon crept into the night sky. Delicate, trembling, but growing in strength, gracefully she took her position amongst the stars. We lit the fire. The dry wood crackled and blazed bright within Rowan House, making the world outside the walls seem suddenly darker. Annie raised a silent toast and we drank to the Midsummer moon with sweet blackberry wine.

"I'll catch a chill if I stay up here. Reckon I'll get back to the house. You coming?" she asked.

"No. I think I'll stay up here a bit longer."

"You planning to see Midsummer in? It's a long night to be alone on the hill."

"I'll stay up here for a bit, see how I go. Don't worry about me. You get some rest." I hugged her bent body, pulling her more upright in my arms.

"I'll be alright." She smiled, straightening herself a little. "I got you looking after me, haven't I?"

I watched her hobble down the slope, back to her dark cottage.

I stoked up the fire and sat with my back against a wall, hugging my knees and watching bright sparks drift upwards until they extinguished. The light of our hilltop fire would be seen from far across the valley. The charm that was meant to protect us also exposed us. My face was scorched by the hot embers but my body shivered. Whoever was after Annie expected us to crumble, to leave the house and the hill undefended. Annie seemed resigned to wait for their next move. I did not want to wait. I wanted to act. I stood up. If only I had some proof. I'd tried scrying for answers but it hadn't helped. I hadn't seen anything. All I had were suspicions. From out of my pocket I pulled a full handful of the black henbane seeds.

I hesitated, remembering what Annie said: 'In the wrong hands, even healing herbs can kill.' Before I could change my mind, I flung a handful of seeds into the fire. They hissed. A sour smoke wafted towards me and I drew it deep into my lungs.

I began to circle the fire. I walked fast around the perimeter, again and again, staring into the depths of it and trying to clear my mind. I picked up my pace and began to jog. With every thud of my feet, I felt myself more able to shut off the babble of my own brain. Perhaps the henbane was taking effect. My heart beat as loud as a drum and I began to sweat. My feet wore a circuit around the flames; my body was leading me now. The fire flashed past; there was only me and the guiding light and a great world of blackness beyond. My eyes glazed. The fire would lead me to an answer. What was real and what imagined, I no longer knew. The faces of Annie's persecutors crowded out of the darkness, daring me to name them as I passed.

The Tremayne men, with their dark, sullen faces, skulked in the shadows, flanked by village boys, their pockets stuffed with plums. Oliver Jenkins, the owner of the chicken farm, stood arrogant in the shadows surrounded by hired men; he tipped them the wink and they moved to do his bidding. Leering into the light I saw Wadsy, angry because I'd rejected him, capable of real devotion and casual harm. He was gabbling silently, justifying and forgetting all at once. And then, moving up the hill, another figure. I recognised the broad shoulders and the dark fall of fringe that hid an angry face. Where *was* Robert? My feet fell with rhythmic fury.

Suddenly a figure stepped out of the darkness, and I halted in my tracks to face them. So they had come. For a moment I stood confused, the light spinning. "You." I mouthed, before throwing myself at the figure in a fury, using all my pent-up rage and grief to pummel and kick and scratch his face. I tore at his hair, throwing up dirt and stones, whatever I could lay my hands on. "How could you!" I screamed. He covered his head from my blows so I picked up a stick and beat him with it. I managed to connect with a few hard thrashes before he took me by the wrists and held me, still kicking, at arm's length.

"Stop. Stop right now!" Robert commanded me, and when I wouldn't, he hooked my leg from under me, flipped me onto the ground and sat on me until I stopped struggling.

"Have you gone mental, Liv? You nearly killed me. What's going on?"

His eyes were wide with shock and I could see beads of blood scoring his forehead where I'd whipped him with my stick. I had been so sure of his guilt. The fire had brought him, hadn't it? Now I wasn't sure of anything. I turned my face to the earth, ashamed. Robert got off me and rubbed a hand across his brow. "You're dangerous, girl." He grimaced. "I want answers, right now."

So, as the fire banked down and the moon rose, I told him the whole history of Annie's malicious stalker. I told him all about Rose Tremayne, the woman who had died in childbirth, not the gossip he'd heard but the real story. And I told him about Nell.

"The deerhound, the big dog? Oh, I'm sorry, Liv. I saw when I came to the house that you were attached to her. But you thought it was me that killed her?" His face went cold as he realised. "How could you think that of me?"

"For all I know, you believe that stuff the Tremaynes have put about. I've seen you fighting. I know what you can do. And after your row with Annie, you suddenly disappeared. What was I meant to think?"

"Yeah, well, I had to get away for a bit." Robert scowled.

"And Wadsy turning up at the farm? Thanks for that. You could have just told me you didn't want me around anymore."

"What? That's not why I offered him a job, Liv. You and Sadie, you just write him off as a headcase. He's not. It's an act. Gets him off the hook. If you'd met his dad, seen his bruises, you'd understand. He's as savvy as the next bloke, believe me, and he's a bloody good worker to boot. So what if he fancies you? It's not a bloody crime, is it? He'll get over it, I expect. Anyway, with you going back to college, we'll need someone else to help."

"With the pig farm?" I retorted.

"Maybe. With whatever happens to the farm. Look, he needed the work. He's not much of a friend, but I've known him since we were kids. This way, at least Mum can keep an eye on him. He owes me one, so he won't misbehave. You gonna spend your whole life keeping your head down, avoiding Wadsy just 'cos he made a pass at you and you weren't interested? Blimey, girl, if he ever tried it on, from what you showed me tonight, he wouldn't stand a chance."

"Sorry," I said, forcing a smile. "So, where were you?"

"I had to get away for a bit. Had to get my head together. I went to stay with Wadsy's brother in Exeter but I've just come from Dad's now. We had a big talk about the farm. We're agreed. There's gonna have to be changes, and I just gotta work out which way they're gonna take us."

"Well, I hope you make the right decision," I said carefully.

"'Spect I will," he sniffed.

Robert helped me build up the fire again. It was getting colder. I huddled as close to him as I could, being careful not to touch.

"I saw the bonfire from our place, thought it must be you two. I wanted to say sorry to Annie," he said.

"She'll be asleep now. I was going to go home myself, but I think I might wait up until dawn. It's only a few hours away."

"Mind if I stay with you?" he asked.

The moon was bright and clear over our heads. I remembered something. I put my hand in my pocket and pulled out a handful of seeds. I held them out in the flickering light for him to see.

"What's that?" Robert asked.

"Henbane," I told him and explained.

He looked thoughtful. Gently, he took my hand and tipped the seeds into his.

"Henbane, huh? Well, I could do with some help seeing which path to take." His eyes locked with mine and I realised he was still holding my hand. "Shall we?"

I nodded. Without taking his dark eyes off me, he flung the seeds into the fire. We breathed deep. Soon I could no longer focus on his face. My eyes closed. Before I slipped into sleep, I felt his hands lower me to the ground and the warmth of his body lying next to me.

We were foxes. We slipped through the low grass; I felt it brush my tummy as I crouched, pricking my fine ears upright.

I was alive to the world. My sensitive snout sieved the night air; my whiskers conducted the smallest vibration. I could hear the tiniest sounds now, the scrabble of a shrew, the flap of a bat wing. In the dark, smell was my vision, the rotting bloom of a fallen fruit, the sour smell of a beetle. I rooted and crunched, my belly scorched with hunger and, suddenly, he was there and an animal joy leapt through me. We hunted together, bounding silently through the undergrowth, chasing each other in the moonlight on the open grass. He pounced and I ducked; we rolled over together, play fighting. I took the scruff of fur behind his neck and nipped him, and he batted me away with a soft paw and a growl. The crushed grass was full of flowers and herbs; it smelt good and I lay on my back and luxuriated, flexing my supple spine as I rolled the hay scent all over myself.

He sat panting, nose twitching to the night breezes. I heard a rustle and a rabbit bolted from the grass. Without thinking I flipped myself up and lunged. It tried to turn but misjudged the angle and my jaws closed around its neck. I felt my teeth puncture fur and skin and a flood of satisfying warm blood filled my mouth. The rabbit kicked twice and then was still; I took its skull in my mouth and my long canines popped through the bone to soft brain beneath. I used my paws to hold the rabbit's body as I stripped it of its fur. When I had eaten my fill, I shared the rest.

Suddenly, the sound of a hunting horn. And we were off, slipping low through the brush thicket, squeezing our narrow bodies through tight spaces, weaving in the darkness. The thundering of hooves was right above us and the bay of hounds blocked out thought. Survival, that was all. I would fight; I would not lie down like prey. I snarled and fought as a hound found me out, and I caught her hard by the lip, ripping the soft skin and sending her yowling before I turned and fled. He was with me, racing through the darkness, racing for the cover of the soft earth with our bellies full of meat. We curled up together, twining our tails, winding our sinuous bodies around and around until we found comfort, each resting their head on the other's silken fur, then we slept.

31 – Burn Them Quick and Burn Them Slow

I woke up just before sunrise, lying next to Robert. I could feel
the rise and fall of his breathing. He was still asleep, his arm
wrapped protectively round me. He smelt of wood smoke and
hay, and he was warm. I lay very still and tried to recall my
dream. The hunt, the prey. It had all come from me. I was the
fox and the hunter. I looked up slowly to study Robert's face.
In sleep he looked peaceful. His hair had fallen from his face;
his dark forehead was smattered by even darker freckles, but
high, near the hair line, the skin was pale. He was so beautiful.
I wanted so much to run my finger through his hair, to kiss each
one of those freckles, but I didn't want to wake him, to return
to our old awkwardness. I soon grew so cold and stiff that I had
to move. Very gently I flexed one foot.

He woke with a start, and seeing me awake quickly removed
his arm and sat up. "What time is it?" he croaked.

"Nearly dawn, by the looks of it," I said, leaping up,
stamping to warm myself and raking up the ashes of our fire.

The moon had gone, the stars were fading and a grey light
was gathering in the east. The sky was tinged with pale
primrose yellow then warm apricot.

"Midsummer's Day," I remembered, lifting my arms and
stretching to greet the sun as the world rolled towards it. The

first rays of sun glimmered over the horizon, making us squint. Robert stood up to greet the day with me.

It was Robert that spotted it first, the way the light caught the rowans one by one, telling them off like hands around a clock, illuminating the tree tops so they shone in the reflected glory of the solstice sun. Thirteen trees. It had never occurred to me before. One for each moon of the year. And as the sun rose, it entered into the central structure of the rowan ring, the fallen house, striking it face-on until the stones themselves seemed to burn with a fire of their own. I felt the power returning to the hill. It came stealing with the dawn, creeping over the hill in a wave so powerful that it made all the hairs on my body stand up straight. Robert was grinning with amazement, lifting his arms to the majesty of the sun.

"Can you feel it?" I yelled, my eyes blazing with the sweetness that pumped through my blood.

"I can feel it!" he whooped, jumping from foot to foot, unable to contain the brilliance of the light that flowed into him, through him, from him. We were beautiful. The stones were charged again, the earth throbbed with solar energy. Whatever influence had drained them had gone, for now, and we had just watched the alignment of earth and fire. This was what our ancestors had seen, this was what they felt here. This power was the reason they had put standing stones where now the rowans stood. Whatever meaning they took from the way the light painted the circle and its central tower was now lost, but I knew why they came. This was where Annie's grandmother had greeted Midsummer. Perhaps it was her who had planted the rowans as saplings. She would have watched from the window of the cottage. Her husband had built it to hide the shame of his wife's weird thanksgivings – to silence the village gossips who called her a witch in the marketplace, then came creeping at night for charms. The light had moved down the walls now, the trunks of the rowan trees were lit up. Robert was exhilarated. He moved between the trees, chasing the light, placing his hands on the glowing bark, and chuckling as he felt the light warm them.

At last he returned, panting, and gazed out over the valley with his hands shielding his eyes. "I ain't never seen nothing like that before. I can see the whole valley, look, there's our farm. That sparkle in the distance, that's the sea even. Sounds stupid, maybe it's that henbane talking, but it's like it's all been blessed," he murmured.

"I'd forgotten just how blessed we are," I smiled.

We sat for a while, contemplating the sun. The bonfire had burnt itself out, but there was still a strong smell of smoke in the air. Acrid, chemical smoke, wafting up from the valley. We scrambled to our feet in unison and both began to pelt down the hill.

Annie's cottage was on fire.

Robert had to break the door down. We plunged into thick, black smoke, the kind of foul, poisonous fumes that come from burning foam.

"I'll get Annie. You get the dogs!" Robert shouted, rearing back for breath. Then he was gone, taking the stairs two at a time.

I found Noggin and Pip cowering in the corridor that led to the still room. There must have been just enough of a draught for them in there. I tucked one under each arm and dived through the black billows to the welcome air outside. The dogs huddled close to each other, licking each other's eyes and noses. I was bracing myself to enter the cottage again when Robert appeared in the doorway. He was carrying Annie's limp body in his arms. He buckled at the knees, placing her on the wet grass and coughing out the fumes. I shook Annie's shoulders and called her name. I stroked her hair and wrapped her in my coat. Her body felt as frail as a bird's; I could feel all the knobbles on her spine.

"She's unconscious. Call an ambulance," Robert croaked.

I had to run up the slope to get reception. My fingers could hardly find the buttons on my mobile phone. Robert had his ear to Annie's chest. Her face in profile was scary; she had taken her false teeth out before bed and her mouth drooped open. Her skin was taut and yellow looking. She seemed so small.

"Please don't let her be dead," I prayed wildly to anyone who might be listening. While Robert and I had been chasing the sunlight on the hill Annie had been suffocating in her bed.

"She's breathing," he announced. "But I don't like to think what she's breathed in."

A woman answered and asked me what service I required. When the emergency services were on their way I knelt by Annie's head. "Annie, can you hear me? The dogs are okay, the house is going to be alright. I want you to stay strong for me, keep breathing, yeah? You just hang on."

From somewhere, I found the strength to support her. Robert had recovered a little. He ran off to get a hose-pipe.

The worst bit was watching them drive away with her. They wouldn't let me in the ambulance because I wasn't family, and because I was too young. They lifted her onto a stretcher and, with blue lights flashing, they carried her off to hospital. Just then, several firefighters came running; the fire engine couldn't get up the track. They took over from Robert with the garden hose. One of them checked him over and gave him some oxygen.

"Annie never lights the fire in the living room in the summer," I told Robert.

His brown eyes met mine over his mask and I saw he'd understood. Just then we heard a police siren.

Jack arrived looking beside himself with worry. "Don't worry about the dogs," he told me in a shaky voice. "I'll feed 'em for as long as needs be."

He looked awful. He was beside himself with worry. His face was flushed, he wrung his hands, and his pale blue eyes were red and bloodshot. I wondered if he'd been crying. I cringed to think that the last time I'd seen him I'd been breaking into his chicken farm.

"My mother, God rest her soul, she'd never forgive me if anything's happened to Annie Tilke," he told me earnestly. "She made me promise I'd keep an eye out for her, and now this. I nearly had a heart attack when I heard the fire engines coming. I told her time and again to watch out for that hearth, and all those candles she had." He wiped a hand across his eyes. "Stubborn old bird, she wouldn't go into a home. Looks like she might not have the choice now."

He ran his hands through his thinning hair, and stood looking at the chaos of flashing lights: fire experts were squelching through puddles of water to take photos of the damage; firefighters carried out the remains of the charred sofa; and a police officer was still interviewing Robert.

I was glad Annie had someone like Jack looking out for her. At least she had one friend in the village. I hated to think of people saying she'd got her comeuppance. I'd said nothing to the police but I decided to confide my fears in him. "I don't think it was an accident," I told him.

"What d'you mean by that?" he asked quietly. He looked shocked.

"I mean, I think someone started that fire on purpose."

His eyes widened as I told him all the things that had happened. "Why didn't she tell me it'd got so bad? I would've been up here with my air rifle. I tell you what, if you're right and whoever did this shows their face round here again, they'll have to answer to me."

With Nell gone, Annie needed a protector. From the look of pain in his eyes, I could see Jack was fiercely loyal to her. He softened a little.

"Once they've checked the house over, I'll stay up here for a bit, in case they decide to come back. They won't try nothing with me here. Tell you what, I got some paint at the farm; I'll get the paintwork sorted for when Annie comes back."

I knew we were both thinking *if* she comes back.

32 – Kiss the Hand of Her Times Two

The police drove me home on the day of the fire. Fortunately, Mum was out, but Dad was furious.

"You're not even sixteen, Olivia. You're too young to be out alone at night, and especially in the company of that young man. If he's laid a finger on you …"

"It's not like that, Dad. We weren't—"

"I don't want to know. You're underage. If the police chose to look into this you could find your precious boyfriend getting arrested."

"He's not my boyfriend. Arrested for what?"

"Don't make me spell it out. Oh, for God's sake, Olivia, tell me you used precautions!"

It took me some time to convince Dad that I hadn't been having sex with Robert. It embarrassed me even to think of it. Dad couldn't understand why I'd wanted to see the sunrise and I wasn't about to tell him. In the end I promised that, at least for the time being, I wouldn't go out at night. Dad said he'd play it down when he told Mum.

The next day, feeling spongy and sick with fear, I went to the hospital to see Annie. I didn't like hospitals much: the floral disinfectant that masked more putrid body smells, the waft of cabbage from the canteen, the sharp smell of surgical alcohol.

The geriatric ward was at the back of the hospital, removed from the more cheerful business of mending broken legs and scanning pregnant bellies, so as not to depress anyone. My trainers squeaked on the shiny grey lino as I made my way down the long corridors to where Annie lay.

When they showed me to the ward, filled with other ill, old ladies, I didn't recognise her at first. Her eyes were closed and they told me she wasn't properly conscious. Her bare arms lay on the white sheets, bones hung with wrinkled flesh and flecked with mustard-coloured age spots. Her face was hidden with a greenish oxygen mask, and bruises bloomed on her wrists where they'd put the tubes in. I held her cold hand, stroking the papery skin that covered her blue veins and feeling the soft pads of her fingertips.

"There's a lot of congestion in her lungs," the doctor told me. "We're doing tests to see how much of it is smoke damage. She's also got a chest infection. I imagine that's been ongoing for some time, caused by the damp conditions she was living in. We just need to check there's nothing more sinister going on in there."

"You mean lung cancer?" I asked, cold dread in my belly.

"As I said, we won't know until the test results come back," he breezed.

I visited every day after school but there was no change. She was still weak, drifting in and out of a deep sleep. Then, one day, just as I was entering the hospital, my mobile phone rang.

It was Robert. "Liv, that you?" he said. He sounded scared.

"What's the matter?"

"Listen. I found something out. Might be nothing, but, even in hospital, I think Annie's in danger."

The minute I heard what he had to say I started sprinting. Even here. I had to get to her. But the hospital was like a maze. I must have been on the wrong floor; the layout was the same but nothing else was familiar.

"Oi! No running in the corridor," a porter shouted after me.

I ignored him, dashing on, dodging trolleys and wheelchairs. I found a flight of stairs and raced up it, two at a time, before barging through the double doors of the geriatric ward. At the end of the long ward a woman was leaning over Annie, about to inject something into the canula in her arm.

"Stop!" I shouted, and the woman turned to face me.

She had been a young woman when I saw her in the dark waters of the scrying bowl. But although she'd dyed her black hair blonde, I recognised those dark eyes, that snub nose. She was Rose Tremayne's sister-in-law, the girl who'd helped with the birth. Her mouth pursed with disapproval as I raced to the bed. She put down the syringe and planted her feet. Annie's purple lids were closed, but I could see her chest rising and falling. I'd got there just in time.

"Young lady, this is a hospital. I will have no shouting on my ward."

"I saw what you were going to do. What's in that syringe?" I challenged. Nurse Baxter, her name tag called her. I knew better.

"Do I need to call security?" she threatened. "I don't know quite what you're accusing me of, but for your information this syringe contains antibiotics. Antibiotics to help your friend here recover from her chest infection. Now come away from the bed and we'll talk about this properly in the visitor room."

I allowed her to lead me away by the elbow but only to get her away from Annie.

"I know who you are," I said when the doors closed behind us.

"Do you, now? And are you going to introduce yourself?" she asked sarcastically.

"I'm Olivia White. I'm a friend of Annie's. If you've done anything to her ..."

"Done anything to her? We're all concerned about helping Mrs Tilke get better."

"Yeah, right. You must have got a surprise when you saw her in your ward. The perfect opportunity to get your own back," I hissed.

"I don't know what you're talking about." The woman faltered. Those brown eyes had the same wild look as before. The years had not been kind to her; she was fatter now and the blonde perm looked artificial above her dark brows. My heart was pounding and I felt light-headed. I had caught her in the act.

"You've got her at your mercy in here. Your family have turned everyone against her, hounded her, worn her down. I don't suppose you think anyone would even notice if an old lady in your care passed away. Well, I've seen what you're up to, Nurse Tremayne."

"How do you know my maiden name?" The nurse gaped, staring at me blankly for a few moments, then she shut her mouth and clicked back into professional mode. "Well, Olivia. You've made a lot of accusations today. I think it would be a good idea if first we both calmed down. If you like, I'll ask my colleague to show you what I was about to inject Mrs Tilke with, so you can see for yourself. And then perhaps you'd like to ask Annie how she is when she wakes up. She was quite bright this morning when my shift started. She's been asking for you."

Annie could only speak in short bursts. She still needed to draw breaths from her mask. But her face looked pinker now she was awake and she'd sat herself up. She reached out her frail stick arms when she saw me coming. I rushed to her, and fearing to crush her if I hugged her, I took her hands and kissed them instead.

"The house …" she wheezed.

"It's fine. Not damaged. Jack's been fixing it up for when you get home."

She waved the idea away. "Gotta build up my strength first … He's a good boy …" She put the mask on for a few moments. "Animals?"

"They're all well. Don't worry about anything. Me and Jack will manage things."

I didn't tell her that Jack's work on the chicken farm was making it hard for him to tend to her animals. I'd been popping in during the days. How would we cope when term started?

Nurse Baxter asked a doctor to explain Annie's antibiotic medication to me. There was good news on her test results: the smoke damage was minimal, and there was nothing more sinister than a bad chest infection. I apologised to Annie's carer.

"Sometimes when you're worried about someone, emotions can run high," she replied understandingly. "Now, I'm getting to the end of my shift. If you're up to it, Mrs Tilke, I think we need to have a much overdue chat about what happened all those years ago."

Rene Baxter, formerly Tremayne, did all the chatting. Annie just squeezed my hand, her eyes unfalteringly locked on Rene.

"Oh, yes, I know Mrs Enticott, though I can't say I've seen her since we moved away from the village. It was her who told your friend Robert I worked here? Well, that solves that one. Yes, Baxter's my married name. I got married soon after Rose died, then I started my nursing training when my children were at school. D'you know, I think it was because of that awful night that I went into nursing. That sense of utter helplessness, I never wanted to feel that again. I couldn't do a single thing to save her. No one could, though, Lord knows, Annie here tried her best.

"Rose already had five children, too close together for her own good, if you ask me, but you know how these farming families can be. More children to work the farm. Except Rose only ever had girls, and Roy, that's her husband, my older brother, wanted a son. Well, he got one in the end. The boy that died. She'd not felt that baby move all day, and she was worried. I told her to get to the hospital, but Roy told us we were being silly, that the baby was probably just asleep and the doctors would likely send her home again. He talked her round. The snow had started falling then, but she said she just wanted to get the little ones in bed before they set off. The contractions were coming close together then. That's when I went against Roy and called Annie. Just as well I did. By the time she got there it was too late to get to the hospital; we were pretty much snowed in.

"It's my belief that the baby could not be saved. I think he was already gone. Cord around his neck, most likely. He was a big baby and that's why the labour was so hard for her. From what I learnt in my nursing training, I think Rose must have had a stroke as well as all that blood loss. But Roy, he never could accept it. I think he felt guilty. I know he said some terrible things after it happened. I can't believe anyone ever listened to him though, least of all his own family. It was plain he was just grieving for his wife and looking to make some sense of it all. Roy passed on three years ago. To think that Mrs Tilke here's had to suffer from spiteful gossip and worse. I can't believe they'd do such things but still, as soon as I can, I'll talk to them. Talk some sense into them after all these years. I was there, and I saw what happened and I'll put things straight. Don't you worry." She turned on her cheerful nursing voice as she squeezed Annie's hand. "You've got nothing to be ashamed of, Mrs Tilke."

There it was, forgiveness. Annie let go of me to pat the nurse's pudgy hand with her own bony one. Nurse Baxter left us alone. I stroked Annie's back as she turned to the wall and closed her eyes against the tears.

33 – Lest Ye Love Be False to Thee

Three weeks later, Annie tottered towards me across the breakfast room of Tree Tops Nursing Home. "Livia," she cried, in a pitiful little voice, "you've come at last. You've come to get me out of here."

Her eyes were red-rimmed, and although there was colour in her cheeks, it was a flushed, unhealthy colour. Standing in the doorway, I cowered back and was relieved to feel the warm bulk of my father behind me. I was so grateful he'd offered to come with me. I couldn't do this alone. It must mean he was a little better.

I couldn't meet Annie's eye, but as I flashed her a tight apologetic smile, I saw her hope extinguish. A hard, dead look came over her face, and she sneered, "I had high hopes of you, Livia. Shoulda known it though. You're just like all them others. Think you know what's best. Well, I tell you, I ain't staying here much longer, even if it means leaving in a box. I seem to remember you saying you wouldn't leave me again, but that was just a lie, I suppose." Fiercely, she turned away from us and scowled out across the lawns of the home to the sea beyond.

As soon as she was well enough to leave the hospital, they had transferred Annie to the home, but according to Frances, the big, patient home manager, she had made every second hell for her carers.

"Why can't I go back? What's wrong with me?" Annie would snarl at them. "I ain't dying, am I? Then you ain't got no right to hold me here against my will. I ain't gonna rot here, turn into a zombie like them others. I want me animals, and my own things. I lived alone for thirty years, don't think I can't manage by myself. Don't you patronise me, young woman. No, I don't want a bloody biscuit!"

I hated to think what Dad was making of her. It wasn't the best of introductions. So this was the woman whose company his daughter had been keeping all this time, her teacher, her friend? But he put his hand on my shoulder and gave it a squeeze, steering me into the room.

Annie sniffed dramatically and turned her back on us.

Tree Tops Nursing Home was in Seaton. Gulls wheeled in the blue sky above the red cliffs, and the little Victorian houses on the promenade had looked quaint and seasidey as we drove past them. Watching the families on the pebbled beach with their fish and chips and ice-creams, it had been an effort to remember how bleak the town was in winter, how the cold, brown waves surged towards the concrete sea-breaks, how the town battened down, damp and shivering against the gales.

The home was in a big white converted mansion house, and, true to its name, it was surrounded by tall pine trees.

"You won't be wanting those cardies," Annie's carer Frances had laughed at the door as a great gust of warm air hit us. "They feel the cold, the old folk. It's always like a sauna in here."

As she'd led us down the corridor towards the day room, I'd got a strong smell of air-freshener, but beneath it, cooked mince, leaking incontinence pads, something clinical. Around the edges of the day room, high-backed chairs were gathered around a distant telly; some TV chef was explaining how to make a pudding. There was a lot of laughter from the studio audience. The volume was too high for anyone to have a conversation, but I hadn't got the impression any of the old people were listening to the programme. They were mostly women, sunken eyes, necks thrust forward, bony chests concave, busts dropped down to waist level. Several residents had craned their necks towards us, but there was no light in their eyes.

"Good morning, lovely day!" Dad had said in a loud, cheerful voice, while I had ducked and grimaced.

Annie hadn't been in the day room, but sulking in the breakfast room where we now sat. She was still resolutely ignoring us.

"I'll get you both cups of tea," soothed Frances. "Give her a bit of time," she whispered. "She's talked of nothing else but seeing you, Olivia."

"I'm Peter, Olivia's dad. It's a pleasure to meet you at last, Mrs Tilke."

Silence.

"As you know we've only recently moved to the village; I understand you've lived there all your life?"

Silence.

I bit my lip. Dad was trying so hard. Unlike my mum who always sounded insincere when she was talking to strangers, Dad had a natural ease. No wonder he'd been such a good police officer; it would be hard to take offence to my dad. I reckon he could break up a riot with a few well-chosen words. I was proud of him and I was getting frustrated with Annie.

"Pip and Noggin send their love, Annie," I told her. "And Beryl and Mavis. You should see what Jack's done to clean up all the mess from the fire. He's been painting everything beautifully. You'd never know. No word yet from the police or the fire brigade on how the fire started though."

She refolded her arms across her chest and stared out of the window but I wasn't going to give up.

"The chickens are laying well, and the strawberries are getting ripe." I reached into my bag and pulled out a punnet of strawberries I'd gathered that morning.

I saw her glance towards the table and, beneath her scowl, I saw a look of such longing to be back home that I forgave her everything. I pushed back my chair and stumbled over to her. I wrapped my arms around her and felt her frail body release into my hug.

"I just wanna go home, Liv," she whispered. "I ain't meant to be here. It'll kill me to stay here. I need to be near the hill. I can't sleep for worrying. It's all I can think of. The hill's unguarded. I know I ain't strong enough, but if I could just get up on top, I reckon my strength would come back. Have you felt anything, Liv?"

I glanced over at Dad but he had picked up a paper and was making a great show of examining it, embarrassed by our show of affection, probably.

"It's alright, Annie," I reassured her. "Rene's going to have words with the Tremaynes. All that business is going to stop. Everything seems peaceful."

"The bees?"

"No, but they'll come back, I'm sure. Maybe they're waiting for you to get well first."

"I don't reckon I *can* get well in this place. This kind of place makes you forget what it's like to be alive. Makes it easier to die, then."

"Oh, stop being miserable," I chided, feeling insincere. Personally, I couldn't wait to get out of this suffocating place, and I was only visiting. "You're not going to die. You're going to eat all this food they keep putting in front of you and get fat and healthy and come back and walk the dogs on the hill with me, okay? Now, stop being so stubborn. They're nice people, if you'd let them be nice to you."

Annie grinned ruefully. "I been a test to them, I'll warrant. That Frances, she must have the patience of a saint to put up with me. Got her up three times last night to tell her what I think of this place."

"Annie, you didn't."

"Well," she retorted indignantly, "they don't let you open the windows in this place. Say it lets the draughts in. Never heard nothing so stupid. It was so stuffy in my room! I wanted to smell the sea, and I told her so."

"Poor Frances." I laughed. "Now, are you going to be kind to my dad, or what?"

Over cups of watery tea, Annie managed to charm Dad. She asked him about London, and told him the history of some of the old buildings in the village. I was touched to see them trying so hard with each other for my sake.

"Now listen," she told him firmly, laying a bony hand on his good arm. "This girl of yours, she's got a way with animals that I ain't seen before. Do you know that? Don't let it go to waste."

I felt myself blushing red.

"Well, I'm sure that's a big compliment to your teaching, Mrs Tilke," began Dad.

"'Tain't nothing to do with me," Annie cut in tersely. "It's Livia. She's got a gift. You make sure you tell your wife. Better still, bring her up here and I'll tell her myself. Ask her to come, will you? I reckon her and me got off to a bit of a bad start, and I wouldn't want her to think badly of me."

Before Dad had time to answer, Annie's eye was caught by a figure at the door. "Now, who's this? If it ain't Ronald Phillips. Join us for a cuppa, Ronald."

The old man who doddered in turned out to be none other than an old school friend of Annie's from the village.

"Olivia, see if you can't talk some sense into this old misery here," he teased, gesturing to Annie. "She's been turning the air black with her moods and cursing these last few weeks. Spoils my relaxation it does."

Annie swiped at him coquettishly. Dad looked my way with a raised eyebrow and I had to bite my lip. I hoped I wasn't that obvious with Robert.

"Ronald thinks he's in heaven, all these pretty little chits of nurses looking after him, three meals a day and no one telling him he's in the way," Annie said archly. "I told him, when I get out, he'll have to visit me, so he don't forget what real life is all about. I'n't that right, Ronald?"

Ronald patted her hand affectionately.

An hour later Frances came in to tell us it was dinner time. I left them together, with promises I would visit soon, and hugs from Annie to deliver to the dogs and the goats.

"She will get back home, won't she, Dad?" I asked as we drove home through the winding lanes.

He let out a breath. "Best not get your hopes up, Liv. She looks like a strong old thing, and she's clearly a very independent person, but …"

But she *has* to get home, I thought. I need her. The animals need her. More than that, the hill needs her. I believed that now. She'd called herself the hill's guardian. Somehow, she did protect it and the weird energy I thought I felt up there. Without her, the hill would be vulnerable. Anyone who sensed the power I'd felt in the stones would want it for themselves.

Dad dropped me at the end of Annie's lane as the sun was sinking. I had promised Jack I would take the dogs for a quick walk, then shut the chickens up to stop the fox getting them. I took the dogs down to the stream. I had to carry old Noggin through the long grass. I put him down and watched Pip swimming through the hay, appearing and disappearing like a dolphin breaking through the waves. It was good to be out in the fresh air after the recycled fug of the care home.

As we turned back and broke the cover of the trees, Pip stopped short and began to growl. His hackles stood up straight, and he began to edge backwards until he cowered between my legs. I felt my hair prickle and stand on end. Someone was outside the cottage, lurking by Annie's back door. Someone who wore a long black coat or cloak that hid their face from view. I saw the figure peer into one of the downstairs windows.

"Oi! What the hell do you think you're doing," I screamed, charging towards the house. Anger ignited in my brain and I didn't stop to think if it was a good idea, only that I had had enough of this intimidation. "Do you hear me? How dare you come here. You killed Nell. And you could have killed Annie, you bastard!"

The figure reeled backwards, almost stumbling. I saw them turn and break into a run down the lane. I pounded up the field, Pip yapping and snarling by my side. The taste of blood was in my mouth and my heart was banging in my throat. I was so angry, if they hadn't run, I think I could have taken them on. And it wasn't just Annie and the dogs I was protecting, not even the hill. My own future was tied up with this place, and I wasn't going to let anyone take it away from me. I pelted down the lane towards the road, skidding to a halt and trying to work out which direction the figure had run in, but they had already gone, no doubt skulking behind some hedge.

"This is a warning. If you ever come back, if you ever leave anything at the house," I yelled hoarsely, hearing the wobble in my voice, "I promise I'll get the police on you. I've had enough! This is over. Get it?"

34 – The Horned One Rules

I walked home slowly – scared, elated and still shaky from my encounter. I'd shocked myself with the strength of my reaction and only now did I realise how risky it had been. Although nothing had been proven, a person who might have started a house fire, who might even have given Nell poison, wasn't someone to be messed with. But how quickly he'd turned on his heel and run. What a coward! I just wished I'd got more of a clue to who was beneath that stupid cloak. It was a man, not a boy, that much I was sure of. But who? One of the Tremaynes? The sooner Rene spoke to them the better.

To my surprise, when I opened the front door, I found my sister home. Amber was on the couch sobbing, and Mum was hushing and crooning to her.

"It's all lies, what baby Maia's mother said." Amber wept in Mum's arms, delicately dabbing the tears from her mascaraed lashes. "I can't believe they would just sack me. She said I was trying to drive a wedge between her and her husband, that I was flirting with him. I didn't mean to, Mum, honest! She was just so snappy with him when she got back from work, and he needed someone he could talk to. She was so jealous of me being at home with her baby. She couldn't get over the fact that I was the only one who could settle little Maia. Oh, I miss that baby *soooo* much. It's so unfair. I'll probably never see her again!"

That night she turned on me. "How can you be so selfish, Olivia? It's all because of you that my parents are still living in this dump. Can't you see how unhappy Mum is? Have you ever stopped to think how your behaviour is affecting her? I want them to come back to London. Dad's not getting better here, and I need a place to live now. You're tearing this family apart. Grow up and stop dreaming and tell him it's time to go home," she spat.

"I am home!" I shouted, banging my door.

She kept it up for the next week, needling and nagging. Mum preferred to guilt-trip me, looking pale and defeated, dabbing her eyes with a hanky, sighing and taking early nights. One day I couldn't take it anymore. I packed some things into a bag.

"Tell Mum, if she wants me, I'll be at Annie's," I yelled at my sister. I would much rather be alone at the cottage for a few nights than live with Amber for another minute. And, anyway, I wouldn't be alone. I'd have the animals for company.

"Good riddance!" she yelled back.

"You know you're only giving your mother more ammunition against you, Olivia?" Dad said flatly as I left the house. "If your Mum thinks you're getting out of hand, we'll be packing up for London. You know that?"

It wasn't until I reached the end of Annie's lane, when the initial anger had subsided a bit, that I thought with a shudder of the figure in the cloak.

'It'll be alright. Rene must have talked to her brothers by now. Told them the truth. And they're not after me, anyway,' I reasoned. I almost managed to convince myself.

When I got to the house, I rang Jack to tell him not to bother seeing to the animals as I'd be staying for a few days. But he drove over anyway and showed me the work he'd been doing painting out the smoke marks in the living room. Although he'd been to the home to visit Annie just a few days before, he wanted all the latest. He was disappointed to hear there was still no word on when she'd be allowed back.

He hung around for ages, fixing things, asking for endless cups of tea. I thought he'd never leave. Finally, he stood, hovering in the doorway, looking at me through narrowed eyes. "'Tain't safe, a little maid like you, all alone. I worry for you. Take my dog Trixie, just in case."

I agreed, just to get rid of him, but I didn't see the point. I didn't need a guard dog. Perhaps Rene hadn't managed to speak to the Tremaynes yet. When she did it would put a stop to the trouble.

Upstairs on the landing, my phone beeped.

'Need to talk.'

It was a text from Robert. Seeing his name on the screen, my stomach lurched. I hadn't seen him since the fire.

'At Annie's. Come over 9 tonight?' I messaged back and spent the next ten minutes grinning like a fool at the idea of being alone with him.

The summer evening was finally drawing in by the time I had done all the chores and fed the animals. The smell of Lammas bread filled the house; I would treat Robert to fresh bread and Annie's home-made blackcurrant jam.

Outside, the long grass swayed in the hazy evening light. It was too hilly for corn here, but elsewhere across the country, harvest was underway. Annie said there was a god in the corn who sacrificed himself, his blood running red as poppies. Every year he laid down his life so that we could eat; my bread gave thanks to him. Pip licked his lips from his basket and put one shaking paw over the edge. He was too late – Trixie had spotted him; she darted low across the floor, halting halfway as he cowered back. She lay down on the flagstones where she was, never taking those expressionless yellow eyes from him, daring him to venture out.

I had never met an animal I didn't like before Trixie. She was sly, creeping and biddable. All the personality had been trained out of her. She was a working dog, not a pet. I had watched her crawl silently on her belly, almost invisible in the long grass. She was driven by an instinct to obey, and, just like all collie dogs, the urge to herd, to manage.

"Trixie, bed!" I told her, a bit too harshly. She shot me a baleful look before slinking back. I knelt to stroke Pip and he cowered under my hand, all the while looking nervously at the sheepdog. Noggin sighed loudly, laying his head on his paws. He missed Annie.

I turned the crusty bread from its tin and left it to cool. I went to the windows to breathe in the evening air. I could hear the heifers in the low field moving in the long grass, the constant click and chew of cud. The shadows in the oak wood loomed deep; the patient trees breathed out into the fragrant night, inviting me into the dark depths. A warm breeze caressed my skin. I remembered the feeling of waking in Robert's arms and despite myself I felt my stomach roll over. We'd never spoken of it. It was silly to pretend we were anything but friends. He was out of my league, anyone could see that. And anyway, after September, hopefully, I'd be doing my A levels and he'd take over the farm. Our lives would go in different directions. If he decided on his factory pig farm, I wasn't sure I'd want to see him again. So why had I spent all afternoon tidying the house and making him bread? I looked at my watch: 8.45. He'd be here soon. With a start I shut the windows and ran upstairs to check my appearance at Annie's dressing table.

Annie didn't own a single item of make-up, and I hadn't had time to pack any, but I brushed my still-boyish crop with one of her tortoiseshell brushes. Then I pinched my cheeks to make them redder. My nose had freckled in the sun. I bit my lip. It was silly to imagine anything happening with Robert. With Amber and Mum putting more pressure on me to leave, even though Dad wasn't ready, I was on borrowed time. But how could I ever leave Annie? I stared out into the gathering night.

A movement at the far end of the garden caught my eye. A white patch on a cow in the field beyond perhaps? No. Someone was in the low field, making their way towards the house. Robert must have decided to cut across the fields. But the figure was wearing a long dark coat that reached almost to the floor and was carrying some sort of stick. My heart froze. Whoever was moving steadily across the long lawn, I was sure it wasn't Robert. I couldn't yet make out the face. The figure strode nearer. At the sight of its firm intent, my bravery melted. Ice set in my veins; it was getting closer. It was wearing a mask, and the mask had the face of the devil.

Before I had time to react, I heard shouting. Robert was sprinting up the lane. I saw him hurdle the wall from the lane to the garden and charge straight across the lawn towards the masked man. He tried to wrestle the staff from him, but the other man was bigger and fought back. I pushed back from the window and clattered down the stairs.

At the bottom of the stairs, I got a shock. Trixie was blocking my way, crouched as if about to spring, with a sullen, expectant look and a low, rattling growl.

"Trixie!" I commanded, but for once in her life she was disobedient. She showed me her teeth, and I had no doubt she would turn on me if I tried to run. I looked to the window with a pounding heart. The shouting had stopped, and the figure with the staff stood alone. Robert was slumped at its feet.

I had no choice. I made a bolt for the back door. As I lunged for the handle, the sheepdog leapt in front of me again, this time snarling, with her teeth bared and her hackles raised. I was trapped. Suddenly Pippin shot from his bed and launched himself at the bigger dog, catching her unawares. She yelped in pain as he ripped her ear, then retaliated with a savage snap of her teeth. The dogs skirmished in a frenzy of tugging and tearing. I seized my chance and dashed out of the door, locking Trixie in behind me, hoping Pippin could hold her off. For a second, I thought of Robert, lying crumpled on the lawn. It would be suicidal to try to help him. I scrambled up the hill towards Rowan House.

I knew the devil would follow me. Even if I escaped him this time, he would keep coming back until he scared me away or silenced me forever. I had to confront him, face to face, and only at Rowan House could I hope to find the strength to face him.

"Help me," I pleaded to the stones. "I'm coming. I need you!" Though my brain was washed blank with fear, I trained all my thoughts onto those buried stones, willing them to wake and share their power with me as they'd done before. All my own power seemed to have evaporated and I couldn't think what else would save me. I approached the top of the hill, scrambling hand over foot over hummocks of grass, falling flat and dragging myself up again. My legs were weakened with adrenaline, and my lungs were scorched. My eyes had adjusted to the darkness now but I didn't dare to look behind me to see what beast was following.

35 – Mind the Threefold Law Ye Should

Rowan House shuddered with expectation as I stumbled towards it. Even through the sound of my ragged breath and the pounding of my terrified blood in my ears I knew I'd been noted. That same expectant stillness. But would the stones share their power with me?

"Please, please," I begged them. I flung myself against the far wall of the house and almost wept with fear. I didn't try to hide. He would find me. I could see the yellow light of a lantern jerking to his stride. He must have taken it from the house when he found me gone. I could hear him coming for me up the hill.

He came not like a man, but an animal, loping, growling. Behind the mask the sound reverberated weirdly. I braced myself as he crashed through the undergrowth to the clearing of the ruin. His light spilled into the space, filling it with jagged shadows. He stopped still as he caught sight of me. At first, he did nothing but pant. My senses heightened and I smelt him, my nose pricking to the sour stench of sweat laced with the bitter spores of mushrooms: those fly agaric mushrooms I'd seen in the woods, perhaps. I pressed myself hard against the stones; their solidity was the only thing that stopped my terror melting me to water. The man in the mask drew himself up, taking breath. He opened his arms wide like an actor or a priest, wielding his staff as if possessed by his own grandness.

It was then he began to speak, distorted, high, theatrical, with no accent I could place. "Breath and trees … Breath and earth … The same. Coming to me now, yes, coming. Coming to an end. The colours … I see everything. I hear everything. Good, good, it's working this time … Yes. Yes. I can understand the animals. There is no one who knows what I know."

Suddenly he pointed at me with his staff, laughed shrilly, then was scarily still. My ears strained in horror, trying to get some sense from his ravings. The voice was strange but the cast of the words was familiar. Again, the dangerous growl was back. A bitter tone of resentment entered his voice.

"This place. This power. Should have been mine. SHOULD HAVE BEEN MINE. Not ROTTING, in the keep of *her*. Time to go and she wouldn't go so I *made* her. She'll not come back here now, not ever." His voice became sing-song, almost feminine. "I got my henbane and my toadstools, for flying, flying."

He had knowledge of herbs, too, then, and knew about the power of the hill. He raised up his arms as if hovering high above me, then he dropped them down, stamping his feet and pounding his stick hard on the ground. "I feel it too. I FEEL IT TOO," he shouted like a jealous toddler.

This was no devil, this was a man, and his red mask was the same colour as the fly agaric I felt sure he'd consumed. It had twisted his mind. It was him who had been draining the hill of its energy. I placed my palms on the cold walls and felt only dead stones.

"Now this one, the outsider," the masked man breathed. He spoke impersonally, as if I was a piece of furniture in a room, not a living being. "Thinks she's special, thinks she understands something. She understands NOTHING. Not like me. I'll use it. Make us stronger. Bring them down who don't agree. A waste to let the women keep it. Let the man take charge!"

He flexed his muscles unashamedly, luxuriating in his power. "No charm can protect you. I can do anything I want to you. You are nothing to me. Nothing."

Slowly he began to stalk towards me. He wanted me to run; he would take me by the back of the neck like a frightened rabbit, bludgeon me down from behind and leave me lying on the hill. The cold dread of death.

'Make it quick,' I prayed.

But something strange happened to time as the devil came near me. Fear filled my mind with memories: I remembered sprawling in the bracken scared rigid, the first time I heard voices on the hill; I felt the dark expanse of those nights I'd spent listening to my father. But I had changed. I had learnt what it was like not to fear, but to trust. I had known love, and I had learnt to love myself. I had felt the sun, the moon, the great goodness of green growing things. And with that realisation, the sweet spark of life kindled and I felt warmth flood from the walls into the palms of my hands, and the stones began to crackle in anticipation. I would challenge his hate with light and love. I set my feet on the soil and began to drink in the ancient energy that flowed from the buried stones.

He was close enough to touch me now, toying with me. Still I would not let him break my faith. Annie did not believe in the devil and nor would I. I raised my chin and looked right into the sockets of the cheap plastic mask. A furious surge of recognition and betrayal hit me; I could not contain the power of it. Filaments of light fizzed between the walls as it thrust out of my tingling body. The man started back.

"Take off your mask," I told him coldly. "I know who you are."

The figure stood a moment, then began to fumble at the elastic. It fell to the ground. Jack's watery blue eyes fixed on me, their pupils dilated to black holes by his drug.

We stood like that for a moment, staring into each other's eyes. He, Annie's false friend, and I, her true one. How dare he set foot here? The glass-splintered tomatoes, the stolen plums and the witch's mask were all his work. The chicks on the doorstep, the heron's skull and the fire in Annie's house. I saw him sitting, watching Nell die with a smile on his lips.

All those years of persecution. I could feel the outrage building in me and, as it rose, a pale glow, like soft moonlight, throbbed from the walls. I felt the light pulsating in me, too, and I saw Jack's defiant expression falter. Was the magic coming from the hill, or was it me and my defiance that had returned its power? I raised my hand to see that my own skin glowed ghostly white. Jack rubbed his eyes and shook his head as if he could clear it. He snarled at me then, and raised his heavy stick to strike me.

"NO!" I yelled with the full force of my lungs, but the voice that roared out across the hill was not mine alone. Out of my mouth came a noise that was raw and wild and powerful. It was the voice I had heard on the hill the day this all began. I tasted blood and earth; perhaps it was the voice of the stones themselves, the voice of the guardian spirit of the hill. It burst out of me, filling me with its fury and elation.

Just at that moment, a great tide of nature was unleashed. From the walls of the ruin, hundreds of tiny creatures – mice, voles, beetles – surged across the carpet of leaves towards Jack. They milled about his feet, clinging to the long robes he wore and climbing up his body. He dropped his stick and twirled wildly in his attempts to brush them off. In the luminous air, moths fluttered about his face, and long-eared bats dived in and out amongst them, catching his face with their tiny claws and parchment wings.

From far away I heard a low, droning hum that increased in volume until a huge swarm of honey bees poured into the pool of light. They rolled and roiled in the air around him before settling on a branch just over his head. The bough drooped with their weight, and as the bees moved over one another they shone like a great globule of living honey. A badger blundered from its set, charging with its heavy body and knocking him off his feet. Jack was howling now, caught in a dark nightmare, but I couldn't feel any pity for him. The animals didn't harm him, they only swarmed to him. It was pure exhilaration to channel this great power; joy and awe exploded through me as yet more birds and beasts came to see off the intruder.

White shapes in the darkness told me the barn owls had come. They flew from wall to wall, perching then swooping, brushing him with silent wings. Jack scrambled to his feet, hair wild and full of leaves, face smeared with earth. He lunged to make his escape, but a sleek red fox sprang out of the shadows and began to circle him. He backed against a wall and the fox sat on its haunches as if waiting. It was a beautiful animal with a fine, full tail and pointed ears. It did not seem to fear the man, and as I watched, amazed, I saw it pad softly to Jack's feet and sink down, lowering its head onto its paws as if offering itself in sacrifice. I doubted, then, and the light flickered. Was the fox submitting after all? Jack must have sensed my weakening, because his hand darted into his robes and pulled out a shining blade. I saw it flash as, with a terrible shriek of victory, he raised his arm high to strike the animal.

The fox leapt back and Jack's shriek turned to pain as long whips of bramble burst from the blackberry thicket and fastened tight around his wrists. The knife clattered to the earth, and I saw the field mice pull it deep into the ground. Everywhere, I heard a pushing and a rustling as the trees and plants thrust out new buds, fanning them open in his face, raining pine cones on his head. Nature ebbed and flowed in rippling succession as if sped up by camera trickery; under his feet, grass and creepers writhed upwards, withering away then bursting back to life. Bluebells and daffodils sprang out of the bare earth before returning to their bulbs. Blossom swirled down from the branches of the rowans, and ripe berries pattered and splashed at his feet. All the seasons came together; the scent of crushed fruit and flowers mingled with rotting leaves and winter decay.

The brambles were retreating now and pulling Jack into the thicket with them. He staggered forward in his thorny manacles. The fox watched with calm, bright eyes. Tiny creatures came tottering out of the undergrowth: pale yellow fluffy creatures. Jack was sobbing. He tore free from his restraints as the chicks clustered round him, peeping and pecking at his feet. As he thrashed out into the deepest part of the thorns, I heard a splintering of rotten wood. With a high-pitched scream, he disappeared. There was a thud and a splash of shallow water when Jack found the bottom of his prison: the abandoned well. Silence, for a moment, then I heard his muffled shout as he realised he was trapped.

The fox turned from him then and caught me in its gaze; slowly it padded towards me. The power of the stones still throbbed through my body, but the light had begun to ebb. Quickly it thrust its cold, wet nose into the palm of my hand, then it turned and melted away into the shadows.

36 – Live and Let Live

One week later, the bees returned. I was standing in the sun, watching with amazement the steady stream that buzzed in and out of the wooden hives, when I heard the sound of a car in the lane. As the driver unloaded her bags, Annie stepped out, and we stood shyly smiling at each other, sizing each other up. Cured of her chest infection, she looked stronger, younger, more upright. Perhaps she saw a change in me too; maybe she saw the glow I'd felt inside me since I'd come down from the hill, since I knew, for sure, that the hill's power was real. As the car retreated up the lane, I hugged her and felt strong arms hug me back. Pippin burst out to greet his owner. The only sign, now, of his fight with Trixie was a bandaged paw. Noggin waddled out and sat smiling and panting on the doorstep as Annie fussed over them.

"Right. First things first. Make me a cup of tea. Then, tell me everything," she demanded.

In the grey light of the dawn that followed that night, I'd staggered down the hill, afraid of what I might find in the house.

223

"Thank God! Oof, careful." Robert grimaced as I threw my arms round him. He was clutching a bloodstained tea towel to his head. Pippin whimpered and shivered in a corner. "He's alright. Got a few bad bites though. Trixie's gone. Dashed out as soon as I opened the door. No wonder the dogs never barked when Jack paid his visits. They were scared stiff of her."

As I bathed both their wounds, I told Robert what Jack had said. What came next – the animals, the fox, the light that had burst from the stones – for the time being, I kept to myself.

"And then, somehow, he fell into the well," I finished lamely. It didn't sound very convincing.

He looked at me with one dark, unbloodied eyebrow raised. "Better work on that one before the police get here." He smiled wryly.

"But you guessed it was him, didn't you? That's why you messaged me." I said, realisation dawning. "That's what you were coming to tell me." I blushed to remember what I'd been hoping he was coming for. "He had me completely fooled. How did you know?"

"I didn't know for sure. But there were a few things that got me suspicious. First thing was when I was doing the roof. Jack always said it was full of wet rot, but I couldn't see none at all. Only holes where, now I know, he must've taken tiles out, ripped the felt, boards that he must've kicked through to let the rain in. And then there was this time when we were out shooting. There was this great red and white toadstool that Jack got all excited about, saying you got this amazing high from it. We all thought he was having a laugh, but there was something so serious about him then; I didn't like it." He paused for breath. All this talking was hurting his bruised ribs.

"Then, after the fire, Jack started grilling me, asking me what I knew about these threats to Annie, telling me what he'd like to do to the Tremaynes, since it must be them who was making 'em. Something didn't ring true somehow. It was too much. So, I rung up that nurse, Rene, and she told me that both the Tremaynes denied ever setting foot at Annie's. Plus, they'd both been upcountry at a livestock sale on the night of the fire. That was when I messaged you."

He paused. From across the fields, we heard Jack's muffled howling, and then the sound of sirens.

"What are we gonna say?" Robert wondered.

Mum, Dad and Amber came straight over when the police called them, and in their shock, for just a few moments, my entire family, even Amber, held me tight.

"If he's hurt you …" Mum began, looking deep into my eyes for an answer. When she saw I was unharmed she released a single sob. She didn't understand me, but I knew she loved me. Of course, as soon as she could see I was alright, she gave me a right telling-off; I didn't mind. After everything I'd put her through, I suppose I deserved it.

I let them take me home with them that night, but almost as soon as I'd fallen asleep, I was woken by Dad's groans of pain. I sat up, staring into the blackness, wrestling with myself. I knew he wasn't getting any better, not really. He needed help. And he needed to talk, no matter how hard it would be for him.

I switched on the bedside light and pulled open a drawer. I went to his room.

"What do you want, Liv?" He winced.

I took him by the hand and wrapped the length of red thread three times around his wrist and kissed it. "For courage," I told him, and crept back across the landing.

As it turned out, we didn't have to tell the police anything much. Jack had already told them everything. He was still ranting when they hauled him out of the hole.

)O(

"They put him in a secure psychiatric unit, whatever that is," Annie said. "I hope he gets some help in there. Liv, he used to be such a good boy, if you coulda seen him. I can't get it in my head that it's the same Jack that tried to kill you, that left Robert with broken ribs. Do you reckon he really poisoned Nell?" Annie asked with disbelief.

"I do. And don't forget, he tried to kill you, too, in the fire."

"He must have been fair stewing in his hate and envy. His elder brother got the family farm and he got nothing. That started it, I 'spect. He had this place in his sights all along, I suppose. Gullible old fool I am." She shuddered. "To think I planned to leave him the house, and Rowan Hill too. Goodness only knows what he'd a done with it." She shook her head. "I wonder what his mother told him about me? He knew something of the old ways, somehow. And he knew enough about the power of the hill to know he wanted it for himself. 'Spect he thought it'd give him the chance of a bit of power. Oh, stupid boy, eating those mushrooms, messing with things he din't know nothing about."

"Annie, the things that happened on the hill. What if people find out?"

"Oh, bees and badgers, chicks and brambles." She raised an eyebrow and gave me a knowing look. "The ravings of a mad man, wouldn't you say?" She shook her head. "Yes, he knew a little of the old ways, our Jack, but he forgot something important. It might take time, but whatever you do, good or bad, it comes back on you, times three."

As the news spread, to Annie's great joy and surprise she started to receive letters – at first just a trickle, then some days, great bundles of them – from ashamed well-wishers in the village. Some were delivered with baskets of fruit, and promises of long-overdue visits and offers of help with the garden and shopping. Even Oliver Jenkins, Sadie's chicken man, sent a shocked letter, condemning his ex-employee, and a cheque that more than covered professional repairs on the roof.

Autumn

37 – Merry Meet and Merry Part

"You're all packed up," said Sadie miserably, as she peered through my parents' front door at rooms filled with boxes. She looked tanned and healthy. She'd saved some money at the fruit farm and had just got back from a festival she'd been to with Matt, her boyfriend. Her hair had been hennaed and she'd piled it on top of her head and wrapped it with a hippy-looking headscarf. Her face was freckled, and she'd got the new nose ring she'd begged her parents for. She smiled weakly, but the tip of her nose gave her away. It was pink with emotion. I gave her a hug and took her upstairs to my bedroom.

"Judging by how quickly she packed up those boxes, I reckon Mum's been lying in bed every single night imagining how all our stuff would stack together, just waiting for Dad to say it was time to go back to London. She didn't give him much chance to change his mind."

"How're you feeling?" Sadie asked.

I shrugged. If I could have cut out my heart and buried it in the red Devon earth it couldn't have hurt so much as the thought of leaving. How could Mum ever understand? I knew what she liked: clean, neat, safe, same. She'd never know the fierce, raw feelings that filled my aching chest.

"She must have been pleased with your exam results though?" Sadie demanded.

"I think she was a bit put out. Thinks I did it to annoy her or something. I suppose I kind of did. Still, she's agreed to let me do A levels. That's the main thing."

"Ooh, bloody woman! She doesn't deserve you as a daughter. I'd like to go downstairs right now and tell her what I think of her," Sadie growled. "Go on. Do you want me to bitch-slap her? I could have her, in a fight. What do you think?" She grinned mischievously and mimed some elaborate kung-fu moves to get me chuckling, but then dropped her hands to her lap, apparently defeated by the inevitability of my departure. "You'll do your A levels in London, then?"

"Yeah. There's a place all lined up at the local college. Biology, chemistry, physics and maths."

Sadie reached across and squeezed my hand. "Don't give up, Liv. One day you'll be a brilliant vet," she urged, her earnest brown eyes locked on mine. "You'll make it happen. And when you're qualified you can move back and set up a practice in Devon. Be a real country person. I know it seems like ages away, but if anyone can do it, you can."

I smiled weakly. I would have to keep the faith. But to leave the hill, and Annie, and the animals …

After she'd gone, I joined Mum and Dad outside. They were loading the car with boxes.

"We'll drive you to your Mrs Tilke's," Mum insisted.

On the way she was quiet, but Dad was chatty. His hands were on the wheel and, before he straightened his cuffs, I caught a glimpse of something red at his wrist. 'He's still wearing it,' I marvelled.

"It's time I stopped hiding away, and got to grips with myself," Dad was saying. "I'm going to get some help, Liv. Counselling. They say it can really help."

"Well, hope's the best medicine," I answered.

It was good to see him looking so different. I smiled through my gloom but I was grateful that he and Mum stayed in the car, waiting while I said my goodbyes.

Annie's kitchen was warm and bright. She'd made everything sparkle, from the glass bottles on the sill to the brass on the range. Pippin and Noggin grinned from their bed but I could hardly bear to look at them. I was counting down my remaining minutes with Annie.

"I'm out the back!" she shouted. She came in with a crafty smile on her face. She was carrying a box, which she put down at my feet. I felt a bit disgruntled that she seemed more interested in its contents than me.

"Annie, Dad's waiting for me in the car—" I began.

"I know, I know. Your mum champing at the bit to be gone, is she? Well, well, soon enough," she breezed. She didn't sound the slightest bit upset that we were going. I felt my chest constrict and the tears begin to prick my eyes. Annie was fussing with her box. "I got something for you in 'ere. A little surprise. I heard you passed those exams of yours?"

"Yeah," I croaked. "I passed."

"Not just passed. A's all round, I heard. Well, come on then. Don't you want to see what's inside?"

Smiling weakly, I knelt to unwrap the box. Books perhaps, for my studies. The box shook. I looked up at Annie, alarmed to see her stifling a giggle. I unpeeled the tape that held it shut, and suddenly a cold, wet nose pushed through the flaps into my palm, followed by a blunt, grey head with the softest ears I had ever felt. I lifted the warm, wriggling puppy onto my lap; it had loose folds of skin, great big paws, and tiny needle-sharp teeth that were already gnawing my wrists.

"But I can't, Annie. I can't have a dog in London!" I wailed, hugging the puppy to me.

"No. You can't," she agreed solemnly. "And she's a young dog, so she'll need lots of walking. I can't do it. Ah, well. There's only one thing for it. You'll have to stay here."

It took me a second to understand what she'd just said, but even then, I doubted I'd heard her right. "What?" I blurted. Surely, she wouldn't joke about something so serious. But how? How could it be possible? "What about …?" I gestured towards where Mum and Dad were waiting in the car.

Annie knelt next to me, easing herself down with her hand on her hip. "After what happened with Jack, your dad came a few times to see me in the home. A good man, that. I'm glad he's more himself. He brought your mum to the cottage a few weeks ago, to have a look around, like." She squeezed my hand. "We've done a lot of talking and, touch wood, looks like it's all been sorted out with the authorities."

"What's been sorted?" I sniffed.

She smiled softly. "Well, if it's alright with you, they've agreed you can stay."

"Waaaaaaahey."

The puppy skittered off my lap as I yelled out. I hugged Annie so tight she toppled off her knees and we sprawled in a giggling heap on the floor. I jumped up and ran outside. I threw myself at my dad and he wrapped his arms tight round me. "Thank you! Thank you *sooo* much." I grinned.

He spoke to me sternly. "We'll want regular visits, mind. And updates on your schoolwork. The school seem to think you'll manage the workload. And you're to earn your keep at Mrs Tilke's. She'll expect you to help her with the animals and the housework."

I let go of Dad and looked at Mum. She was looking away, across over the fields, fighting back her tears.

"What made you change your mind?" I asked.

She bit her lip and sniffed. I got the impression she'd been rehearsing what she was going to say.

"I know things have been hard these last few years," she began, "And, well, perhaps I've been so busy thinking about my problems, and about your dad, that I never thought enough about you, except when you started making trouble." She was trying to be strong but there was a wobble in her voice. "Oh, Liv, when you came down off that hill, and I saw you surrounded by all those police officers, I was so scared. Part of me wanted to shake you, I was so angry. But there was another part of me that was looking at you and thinking I might burst with pride. 'That's my daughter,' I wanted to say. 'I don't know how, and I'm sure it's got nothing to do with boring old me, but look, that beautiful, brave, independent girl, that's my daughter.' I realised how miserable you'd be if we made you come back to London."

She took a hanky from her handbag and gave her nose a dab. Then she put her capable face back on. "Now, give me a hug, you. We'll have a quick cup of tea then say goodbye. Your dad and I have to be back in London by six, and I want to beat the traffic."

While we were sitting at the kitchen table, Annie slid a big white envelope across the table to Mum and Dad. They read the contents through, looking shocked.

"No, Mrs Tilke. It's just too much."

"For the last time, call me Annie. No arguments. I made up my mind already. It's mine to leave to whom I choose, and I choose Olivia. I know she's still young but I got a good few more years in me yet. And when the time comes, I know she'll look after them better'n anyone," she said, her eyes piercing mine.

"What, Annie?" I asked, hardly daring to believe.

"The house, Livia. And the hill."

)○(

Robert waved as he joined me at the top of the hill. "I heard you're staying with us," he said, sliding down to join me.

We sat with our backs against a wall and took in the valley, bathed now in a low, golden light. The rowans were heavy with clusters of ripening berries. Deep underground, the stones were sleeping, but I knew he felt their faint throb. I knew it filled him with the same wild joy and excitement.

"Hey, I got my exam results. Not as stupid as I look, it turns out," Robert told me. "Looks like I'll be joining you back at college."

I squeezed his arm to congratulate him, realising that I would get to see him every day. I blushed to think how much I wanted it. How much I wanted him.

"But the farm? You wanted so badly to take over the farm. What's your dad say?"

"We've agreed he'll run things for a couple of years on his own, on his terms. No pig farm though, mind."

"And then?"

"I got this idea, Liv. That morning at Midsummer, looking out over the whole valley and seeing it all sort of, connected, that's when it came to me, and then I talked it through with the teachers at school and they seem to think it's got potential. That's why I'm going back to do A levels. Business studies. I gotta find out if my idea will work," he declared.

"What's the idea?"

"Local milk for local people. Produced by small farms who treat their animals well. People'll pay a bit more if they know where their milk comes from. Break the hold of the supermarkets. Get back some of the old ways. After all, the old ways worked for centuries, don't see why they won't now. Your friend Annie showed me that. And in the meantime ..." He smiled secretively.

"What are you planning?" I pried.

"Not me. It were Mum's idea, and I reckon it might just work. Mum and Wadsy have been busy, doing up the bungalows for farm-stays. He reckons her cooking'll get them down from London in droves, and we got the milking parlour and the baby animals for the kids to come and see. Thick as thieves Mum and Wadsy." He chuckled. "She's making him do his resits, though. That's part of the bargain. Brace yourself, but he'll be back at school in September too."

The start of a new term and a time for new beginnings. The wheel was turning. We had stepped up to take our places in life, and each one of us, in our own way, would help to keep the wheel moving.

The light was fading. We sat uncomfortably, wondering what to say next. I shivered and pulled my jumper round my shoulders. "Well, I should be going." I rose, faltering as he reached out and pulled me back, close to the warmth of his body. Searching my face with anxious eyes, he raised one hand to my chin and then drew me to him. Briefly our lips touched, but I could feel his nervousness.

For a few moments we paused, our foreheads resting together, releasing our old friendship and accepting the powerful feelings we had for each other. Bringing my hand up to his face I pulled back and drank him in. I smoothed the stubble on his cheeks with my fingertips. Wondering, I traced a finger over each freckle. Then, slipping my hand into his dark hair, I tugged him to me and kissed him hard. Joy and emotion bubbled up and we broke from each other, hugging close, laughing with relief, then kissing again and again, just to make sure it was really true. When we finally stopped kissing, I lay in his arms, threading my fingers through his and pressing my head to his chest. I could feel his heart racing. The lights of the outlying farms had come on in the valley beneath us, and above us the rowan trees whispered a blessing.

THE WITCHES' REDE – Anonymous

Bide ye the Wiccan laws ye must, in perfect love and perfect trust.

Ye must live and let live, fairly take and fairly give.

Cast the Circle thrice about, to keep unwelcome spirits out.

To bind the spell well every time, let the spell be spoken in rhyme.

Soft of eye and light of touch, speak ye little and listen much.

Deosil go by waxing moon, chanting out the Wiccan runes.

Widdershins go by waning moon, chanting out the baneful tune.

When the Lady's moon is new, kiss the hand of Her times two.

When the moon rides at Her peak, then the heart's desire seek.

Heed the North wind's mighty gale, lock the door and trim the sail.

When the wind comes from the South, love will kiss thee on the mouth.

When the Moor wind blows from the West, departed spirits have no rest.

When the wind blows from the East, expect the new and set the feast.

Nine woods in the cauldron go, burn them quick and burn them slow.

Elder be the Lady's tree, burn it not or cursed ye'll be.

When the wheel begins to turn, let the Beltane fires burn.

When the wheel has turned to Yule, light the log and the Horned One rules.

Heed ye flower, bush and tree, by the Lady, Blessed be.

Where the rippling waters go, cast a stone, the truth to know.

When ye have and hold a need, hearken not to other's greed.

With a fool no seasons spend, or be counted as his friend.

Merry meet and merry part, bright the cheeks and warm the heart.

Mind the Threefold Law ye should, three times bad and three times good.

When misfortune is enow, wear the blue star on your brow.

True in love ye must ever be, lest ye love be false to thee.

These words the Wiccan Rede fulfill: *An it harm none, do what ye will.*

A Polite Request

If you have enjoyed this book, we ask that you take a moment to write a brief review, perhaps on the website where you bought it, or on Goodreads, or a blog. If you prefer, you could simply tell a friend.

We at Blue Poppy Publishing don't have a million-dollar marketing budget or any celebrity friends, so we rely on word of mouth to tell others about us.

Please be honest. We are not asking for insincerity, although if you didn't like it, a reason would help others. What you dislike might be exactly what another reader is looking for.

Thank you.

About the Author

Alice Allan grew up in rural Devon and, although she has lived all over the world, her heart is still there. She has worked as an actor and narrator, public health specialist and writer.

Her first novel, *Open My Eyes, That I May See Marvellous Things* (Pinter and Martin, 2017) is set in Ethiopia and won the 2018 People's Book Prize for fiction. Her other books for teenagers include *Sugar, Sugar*.

She currently lives in Surrey with her husband, two daughters and a large Ethiopian street dog called Frank.